MOUNTAINS
of
MANHATTAN

jenny lind schmitt

Vinavant Press

www.jennylindschmitt.com

First Edition, Second Printing

Book cover design by Peter at BespokeBookCovers.com

ISBN-13: 978-0997535914
ISBN-10: 0997535911
XV

For Manu, the patron of my arts

Chapter 1

At the corner of 45th and Madison Avenue, Helen slowed her stride. While the sidewalk where she walked was now in shadow, the rays of late afternoon sunshine still shone on the tops of the buildings all around her and made them glow against the clear autumn sky. The breeze floating up 45th Street mingled the watery smells from the East River with the grit from the street and the tangy odor of hot dogs from the stand one block over. This was the scent of the city distilled, and Helen inhaled deeply. In this moment, she was extremely pleased with herself, with her life, with the world. Glancing behind her, she surveyed the smartly dressed stream emerging from the gray building that housed the Committee offices. The ladies in the secretarial pool were pulling on their gloves as they walked out the main doors held open for them by admiring gentlemen in neat dark suits.

With bemusement, Helen recalled the day not long ago, only a week into her new job, when she had been so flustered and busy that at day's end she couldn't find one of her gloves. In vain she had searched, even scouring Mr. Major's office before finding it neatly filed away in the cabinet. Only three weeks had passed since, but she felt like an altogether different person, capable in her work and self-satisfied in her title as Personal Secretary to the Director of the Committee.

And in honesty, she also felt a great deal of personal satisfaction in having today secured a date to the Committee's Émigré Ball, and that it was with Vladimir the Debonair instead of Ivan the Terrible. She had seen the latter circling like a turkey buzzard the past few days – waiting for a chance to ask, she was certain – but she had successfully avoided conversation with him until this afternoon when it had been too late. She had had to work hard at feigning disappointment when telling him that she already had a date and would be going with Vladimir Demidoff. Ivan had knit his dark brows together and looked so awfully morose as he bowed stiffly and turned away that she had almost felt a pang of pity. He wasn't so bad, she thought, and he was nearly handsome in his dark and brooding way. But that was just it. His heavy features, his gloominess, as though the soul of Mother Russia weighed eternally on his shoulders. It wasn't quite what a girl wanted in a dinner date, and it was the reason she and Pansy had dubbed him The Terrible. It felt dreadfully funny and historic.

Vladimir was everything his compatriot wasn't: suave, cosmopolitan, open and engaging. Though he hinted at a background in the old Russian aristocracy – like most of the émigrés at the Committee — he seemed quite comfortable in the world of today and mingling with modern New Yorkers, one of whom Helen was most gratified to be, especially once he began to show her his attentions and an approving eye. She had hoped for an invitation to the ball and was almost sure of one after Pansy Allen had said he'd come round her desk on Monday to enquire about Helen's plans. Why, then, he had waited until this morning to ask she couldn't say; but once yesterday afternoon she had caught his laughing, pale blue eyes watching her as she made a quick exit upon Ivan's unwelcome entrance into her workspace. It had annoyed her, but when he had appeared at her desk this morning with a bouquet of pink asters, a genuine smile, and an invitation, she had quickly forgotten her grievance.

So with her mind on her plans and her step light, Helen crossed 45th. She wouldn't go down to the subway right away, she decided. It was much too nice out for that. She would walk up to the Lexington Avenue station. The air had the clarity and sharpness of the beginning of September. The heat of summer now past, the light breezes brought refreshment with them, and it seemed that the city itself and everybody in it was breathing a gentle sigh of relief. A fresh lilt filled each commuter's step, and as Helen passed each one, it was not hard to imagine their minds laying their autumnal plans. Her mind turned over her own plans and across her red lipsticked mouth played a slow smile of secret thoughts, which never fails to make an attractive young lady yet more attractive, and which caused the heads of more than one passing gentleman to nod his hat in her direction. Not that she noticed much. Her head was too full of her own thoughts.

Fall was certainly the best time to start adventures. No matter if the calendar called January the beginning of the year; September and the return to clear, crisp days was really when things began. The Jewish calendar had it right. Her arrival in Munich had been in the fall, too, just in time for Oktoberfest and all its revelry and music and dancing. It had been in one of the huge beer halls where they'd gone after the parade that she had first met most of Heinrich's friends. Helen had thought it would always be like that, meeting people, dancing, drinking, laughing. How mistaken she had been, she thought with a touch of bitterness. How differently things had turned out.

But there was no time to waste on thinking of that now. Here was a new adventure in a new city! An American city with no bombed out buildings and half-rebuilt churches. New York City, no less, with no weighty traditions and heavy expectations to ensnare you. She would be only who she, Helen, wanted to be. No more, no less.

She had been walking north, and now nearing the corner at 48th Street, her eye spotted an attractive hairdo on the corner that brought her abruptly out of her reverie. It was a smooth, honey-colored chignon, the kind that always made Helen revert to her childhood longing for blond hair. She had long ago vowed to make peace with her light brown waves, but encountering hairstyles like that brought on lapses. It looked so sophisticated. Wearing the chignon was a young woman about her own age in a lightweight, flattering gray suit, but to Helen's surprise, as she neared she could see the woman was passing out theatre bills. This was the best-dressed theatre bill person she had yet encountered. Helen adored the theatre, and upon settling in New York, had determined to attend as often as her budget would allow. A culture of live theater was an art form of peacetime, and as such, had not been a high priority in a Germany only ten years postwar. She had missed it. As she came to a stop at the corner, she glanced at the pretty young woman and held out her hand eagerly for the playbill.

Bible Study and Benefit Concert for Orphans of the Korean Conflict
Commencing our weekly Fall Study Series on the topic, "Does it matter what God thinks?"
Friday evening, 7:30 p.m., Manhattan Baptist Church.
Soup Supper preceding

Helen felt her smile freeze on her face, but her hand stayed outstretched, holding the offending paper. *No, thank you!* she thought emphatically. Friday night was hardly a time for a Bible study of all things! And anyway, God already had one day a week, and he ought to be happy with that. She thought it more than enough. The orphans, though, goodness, she was sorry for them. Germany had been full of orphans and now here were more in Korea. Still, there was surely a better time for such a thing; facing the woman, she folded the paper as if to show her thoughts and waited for the light to change. It persisted in its redness as the traffic continued to whiz past, and it seemed to Helen that this must be the longest light in all of Manhattan. Glancing around, she saw that she stood alone on this corner with the Bible Study Lady. Inexplicably, all the other commuters in New York City crowded onto every street corner but this one. She stole a peek at the Bible Study Lady. To Helen's horror, the woman's lips parted as if she were going to say something. She was going to make conversation.

Despite the chill in the air, Helen started to flush. She felt a panicked need to get away and glanced at the stoplight on 48th as it finally turned yellow and the last few cars streamed through the intersection. It was good enough. Like a bold city-dweller, she stepped off the curb and away from the impending social interaction. She didn't see the last yellow taxi through the light until it was nearly upon her. With a wild honk of its horn it swerved out into the next lane just in time. In fright, Helen jumped back onto the curb. She stumbled a few steps and fell. As she tumbled to the pavement, she felt the right heel of her new black pumps catch in the subway grate. Her foot pulled one way and her body lurched the other to land at the feet of the astonished Bible Study Lady. Pain burst through Helen’s ankle and up her leg, and instantly, tears shot to the corners of her eyes. For a few stark seconds she sat there in a frightened heap, and then the Bible Study Lady was gently removing her shoe, and then a man in a navy blue suit was patting her ankle, telling her that while he was no doctor, he didn't believe it was broken.

"But you should probably have a doc look at it. Most likely a sprain. I wouldn't go far on it, if I were you. Do you have a ways to go? I'll hail you a cab."

"Oh, no!" Helen cried, "I'm taking the subway." Cab fare at that distance would be beyond her ordinary budget, and for the moment she refused to believe this was an extraordinary situation. With the help of the two strangers, she struggled to her feet.

"But I don't think you can walk," said the Bible Study Lady, doubtfully, as Helen's leg crumpled under her own weight. A fresh wave of tears sprang into her eyes, this time less from the steady throb in her ankle and more from the annoying frustration of being helped by the very person she had just been trying to avoid. For an instant she wanted to blame the Bible Study Lady, *It was her fault this happened! If people would just mind their own business!*

But at least Helen was too honest for that. She had been rude and careless, and her accident was her own fault. More tears threatened to flow, but she stubbornly blinked them away. She took a deep breath and thought a moment. She tersely explained there was a bus that went all the way up Madison Avenue. It would take four times as long, but it would drop her off two blocks from her apartment and there was a stop on the next block.

"I'll walk you there," said the lady. The gentleman tipped his hat, giving his well wishes, and the Bible Study Lady firmly held her right arm. Slowly and gingerly they crossed 48th and then Madison to get to the northbound bus stop. Mercifully, the other woman did not insist on making conversation as they went, but limited her comments to her hopes that the walk was not too painful and her certainty that a good rest at home would set it to rights. Not until the doors on the bus closed did Helen realize that she still held the Bible study flyer crumpled in her hand and felt a trace of shame that she hadn't really thanked the woman at all.

Chapter 2

The bus was nearly full. As Helen hobbled up the steps, a shabby young man who had been sitting on the side bench behind the driver jumped up and gave her his seat. He moved down the aisle a little ways and stood. Helen sank gratefully into the vacated seat and gathered her wits. It was simply amazing how quickly things could go from good to awful. The pain in her ankle, which during the short half-block walk had eased enough for her to hope it had only suffered a twist, now began to throb again in earnest. She longed to be home so she could put it up and ice it. The bus plodded slowly north, like a placid caterpillar with a notion of an appointment at the end of the twig sometime next week.

Helen looked around the bus and caught the eye of the shabby young man. He looked back at her with an open gaze and a quick smile, then glanced away. She saw that he wasn't really shabby, just disheveled. He was tall and lean, and his sandy blond hair stuck out in all directions, as if he had forgotten to comb it for a few days. The image of a dishwashing brush standing up on its end immediately came to Helen's mind. His brown sports jacket was wrinkled, but decent. The rest of the riders were the usual commuters: dark-suited men, a few well-to-do ladies holding Macy's bags and sporting their new fall coats, nannies and their young charges returning home from an outing downtown. Her eyes returned to the Rumpled Man. He seemed the most interesting person on the bus. She forced herself not to think of a dish brush. He had taken an old, red hardback from a worn leather briefcase and was reading, holding the book in one hand, the case in the other, leaning braced against the seat next to him and lurching with every jolt of the bus. Reading like that would make me positively ill, thought Helen. Just watching him made her feel slightly queasy.

The bus inched northward, and now at each stop more people got off the bus than on. At long last, the driver called out, "95th Street," and Helen prepared to descend. She hadn't thought about it until this moment, but suddenly she wondered how she would walk the two blocks to her building, now that her ankle was swollen to twice its normal size. Once she had gotten painfully down the bus steps to the sidewalk, she stood still a moment, wondering what to do. The two blocks seemed very far. She heard someone else getting off the bus, and she turned to see the Rumpled Man.

"Hello," said he, "do you have far to go?"

"No, well, yes," replied Helen, "only two blocks, but..." her voice trailed away as she peered down at her foot.

"Yes, I noticed. Took a beating from the Big City, have you? Was it your boss that did this to you? Fashion? Or simply modern life in general?"

He said this so earnestly that Helen was taken aback and speechless. Then she giggled stupidly and wasn't sure whether she was laughing at his joke or just at his manner of speaking.

"Forgive me," he apologized, "I'm Thomas Lawson. Would you permit me to help you home?"

Helen acquiesced, thinking that despite his odd way of speaking, he couldn't be too dangerous. And besides, she didn't know what else to do.

So they walked slowly up the avenue, past Carpenter's Grocery and Café Voykop and the florist's shop on the corner, Helen leaning on his arm only as much as she felt comfortable leaning on a perfect stranger. She told him how she had sprained her ankle, leaving out the part about hurriedly escaping from the Bible Study Lady. Thomas Lawson told her that he was a student at Columbia University, working toward a Master's degree in history. He had grown up in Portland, Oregon, and they quickly felt the camaraderie of two Westerners in an Eastern city. She related how she had been scarcely a month in the city and about her work in midtown, but since he didn't ask how she'd ended up here, she didn't bother telling about Heinrich. Instead he asked the name of her firm.

"The American Committee for Liberation from Bolshevism. I am secretary to the President, Mr. Major," she said with a note of importance in her voice. Thomas coughed loudly, then carried on coughing. The first bit had almost sounded like a laugh.

"Wow! That's quite a mouthful."

"Yes, that's why we usually just call it The Committee," she said tentatively, unsure if his reaction meant poking fun at her, or even more worrisome, a lack of concern about communists.

"Which has a rather communist ring, if you ask me. The Committee. Hmmm. Don't get me wrong, I am fully against communism, but I had no idea that there was 'A Committee.' What sorts of things do you committee about?"

She relaxed a little. "Well, it's all about the spreading of liberal ideas into the countries behind the Iron Curtain. We transmit radio news broadcasts from Munich so that people in Poland, Hungary, Russia, and the others can hear the real news from the outside in their own language. Their governments don't permit the free press, you know, they're very nasty."

"Ah, the free exchange of ideas, now there's a principle worth believing in. I suppose I'll have to like your Committee, after all," said Thomas Lawson.

By now they had reached Helen's building on East 96th, where Mr. Angelo Bertoli, the doorman, kept guard under the crisp green awning. His round, usually cheerful face looked alarmed to see her hobbling along. He spread his arms out in question. "Ahhhh! Miss Hartmann! What'd you do to your leg?"

"Oh, Angelo, it's just a silly sprain. Mr. Lawson here kindly helped me get home from the bus stop. Is Rose already home?"

"Yes, Miss Whitaker's been home about an hour." He turned to Thomas and with solemnity, nodded, "You are a very good man to help Miss Hartmann."

In his turn, Thomas nodded gravely back, "It's all in the line of duty, sir. I was an Eagle Scout, you know," said without a trace of irony. But his gray eyes twinkled. "And besides, it was on my way home."

Thomas turned back to Helen. "So it's Miss Hartmann, is it? You must be German?"

"Yes," said Helen, slowly but truthfully, "part German." She smiled up into his honest face and they stood looking at each other for a long moment. There was something unsettling in his gaze, but not unpleasant. She turned abruptly to go.

"Well, thank you so much, Mr. Lawson. You've been very kind."

Thomas flourished a bow, twirling his hand in the air above his head, just missing his dish brush hair, like D'Artagnan before the queen. Then he turned and walked back the way from which they'd come. Helen took Angelo's proffered arm, and he escorted her into the elevator and up to the 17th floor.

"Who's that nice young man, Miss Hartmann, with the funny bow?"

"I don't really know, actually. I just met him on the bus, and he offered to walk me home. He's a student at Columbia."

"He's takin' the long way home, I think maybe." Angelo said this quizzically, with a sidelong glance at Helen. They arrived at her apartment door.

Once inside, Rose helped Helen off with her coat and onto the blue secondhand sofa, which was the only piece of community furniture Helen had contributed to their roommate partnership. Everything else had come with Rose. Rose clucked her tongue thoughtfully over the ankle, which was now taking on a beautiful indigo hue, and she quickly brought a bag of ice. Then she disappeared into the kitchen for a bit while Helen tried to apply herself to *The New York Times*. There was an article in the entertainment section about Elvis Presley's upcoming performance on the Ed Sullivan show. Not for the first time, Helen wished for a television set, if only to know what all the other office girls would be talking about.

Rose reappeared bearing a tray laden with minestrone soup and sourdough bread, and Helen cheered up immensely. She again blessed her luck, or providence, or whatever you wanted to call it, for finding a flatmate like Rose. Rose was easygoing, undemanding, a good listener, and, as Helen now learned, exceedingly capable in a crisis. She wasn't exactly what Helen would call a good conversationalist, but she was sensible and quite sensitive to the needs of others. As they ate their supper—Helen on the sofa with her tray and Rose at the brown mahogany table at the other end of the room—Helen relayed her brush with the taxi and her fall, and Rose listened patiently with a furrowed brow and nodded thoughtfully in all the right places. Rose then cleared away the dishes and sat again at the table with a pile of papers in front of her.

Rose's parents owned the apartment building where Rose and Helen lived. If Helen had been a more reflective person, she might have recognized this as the reason her rent was affordable in an upscale neighborhood. Rose's father, George Whitaker, was an engineering professor at Princeton, but his wife, Alice, had inherited a fortune from her family's textile factories. When it dawned on Helen how well-off Rose's family was, she was infinitely pleased. If she wasn't rich herself, the next best thing was being with people who were. Nevertheless, Rose did not openly display her family's wealth, preferring instead to be judged on her own accomplishments and independence. Her parents had bought the building as an investment when Rose began teaching at Clara Barton Academy and offered the penthouse apartment as an affordable way for Rose to live in a nice part of town. Rose's previous roommate had moved to Florida, and she had subsequently placed an ad in The New York Times Classifieds:

Female Roommate Wanted to
Share Spacious Apartment,
Upper East Side

Against both their mothers' trepidations about finding a roommate in the classifieds, Rose and Helen found themselves delighted with each other and had quickly settled into a warm and practical friendship.

They were comfortably silent now, Rose grading fourth grade spelling tests and Helen thinking over her day. The events of the afternoon had temporarily chased Vladimir and his invitation from her head, but now he returned peremptorily to claim his position in her thoughts. Helen had already told Rose a little about him; she wanted to fill her in with the rest of the story. She opened her mouth to speak, but visions of Vladimir's intense pale eyes disappeared and a dish brush came into her mind. She almost giggled out loud at the thought of his ridiculous hair. And before she could stop herself…

"You know, Rose," she began. "I met an interesting man on the bus."

But Rose was between *pneumonia* and *psychology* and did not answer.

Chapter 3

A visit to the neighborhood doctor the next day confirmed that Helen had, indeed, sprained her ankle quite badly. He prescribed some nasty tasting medicine to help with the pain and, much worse, an unwieldy brace to wear for four weeks to help give the ligaments time to heal. In addition to the ankle, it covered half of her leg and foot, and was stiff and uncomfortable. Not to mention, quite unsightly. While she wore it, she was also to get about on crutches. He sent Helen back home to elevate and ice her foot to try to bring down the swelling in the now-ballooning ankle. It was very distressing.

When Helen called Pansy at the office to say that she wouldn't be in tomorrow either, she could tell Pansy was annoyed to have to pick up her slack.

"Mr. Major isn't too happy with you," Pansy confided. She smacked her gum in between sentences. "Remember how I told you he came in to work once with his leg in a cast the day after he broke it?"

Helen did remember, but what could she do? The doctor had told her to rest her leg, and she couldn't do that very well if she wasn't resting the rest of herself. She was actually grateful to have a day of peace from Mr. Major and his incessant crises. Of course she was committed to her job, but The Committee didn't expect her to show up as an invalid, did it? No matter how many casts Mr. Major might have worn to the office? Later, she admitted to herself that she could have taken a taxi tomorrow at The Committee's expense, but she had already made the phone call, the damage was done, and anyway, tomorrow was Friday. Surely they would survive without her until Monday. She passed the day on the couch reading and occasionally hobbling to the kitchen for snacks. At quarter to four, Rose returned home from Clara Barton and again fixed dinner for the both of them before applying her red pen to a stack of history tests in front of her.

Friday afternoon brought a surprise. Rose had just arrived home from work and was bringing fresh ice to Helen, who was well-installed in her place on the sofa, when the doorbell rang. It was Thomas Lawson, the Rumpled Man, looking much less rumpled now, Helen noted. With a freshly pressed blue oxford shirt and his sandy hair combed neatly down, he looked quite presentable. Only a small tuft of hair near his crown still insisted on sprouting heavenward.

He carried a large bouquet of bright pink and orange zinnias "for the invalid," he said as he entered. Helen was taken aback and spluttered how pleased she was to see him. She certainly hadn't expected anyone, and sat with her fuzzy, blue chenille bathrobe wrapped over her shoulders to keep off the chill. It was another fine September day and the doors to the terrace were open, but she had hardly moved for two days and her blood was cold. But if Thomas noticed her casual attire, he refrained from mentioning it, and instead kept his comments on the charm of the apartment and the state of her ankle.

Rose brought tea for the three of them in small, round, brown teacups, and thus began a pleasant half-hour of conversation. Thomas was a conscientious conversationalist, Helen noticed, paying her every attention, but also making an effort to draw out reserved Rose. When he discovered she was a school teacher, Thomas began asking questions about her education philosophy. His Master's thesis, he explained, was on how the mandatory Prussian school system in 19th-century Germany was connected to the rise of National Socialism in the 20th. Thomas grew quite animated, his grey eyes bright as he warmed to his subject. Rose engaged him skeptically, in her quiet way, and Helen—without strong opinions on compulsory education—began to feel left out of the conversation.

Finally she butted in, "Well, the Germans I knew in Germany all seemed quite happy to send their children off to school as soon as they could get rid of them, compulsory or not." It had the desired effect of stopping Thomas mid-sentence in surprise.

Rose filled him in, "Helen, you see, lived in Munich for three years. She's only just moved back to the States, so she has firsthand knowledge about life in Germany." She smiled across at Helen, happy to give her an opening. Helen was pleased to see the impression it made on Thomas.

"Don't tell me you were fighting communists there, too?!"

"Well, technically, I was liberating from Bolshevism," said Helen with a wry smile, "but yes, The Committee has an office in Munich."

"Tell me more, Helen. I've studied about Germany for years, but I don't know if I'll ever get there."

So Helen told him about the Munich she knew. As much as she liked being the center of attention, she wasn't a natural storyteller, but as she spoke, the sights and sounds and smells of the Bavarian city came back to her and she talked on and on. And because Thomas was wistful for a place he'd never been, she focused on the beautiful things that she had loved: the old buildings and archways around Marienplatz, the cathedral with its twin onion dome bell towers. She told them about her acquaintances and their children and their schooling. She told them how the buildings around the Rathaus were now almost entirely rebuilt after the annihilation of the war. She told about buying her fruits and vegetables in the Viktualienmarkt nearby, the air a mélange of the smells of cheese, roasting sausages, fresh flowers, and whatever vegetables were in season.

"It's fall now; they would all have Pfefferlinge," she said, thinking of the pungent orange mushroom. "They set up stands in the street and that's all they sell, and everybody buys them and eats them for three weeks straight. Then the season changes and the stands all sell something else. Oranges in the winter, asparagus in the spring."

Then she told them about the marionette theatre near the market where she had first seen *The Magic Flute*, acted entirely by marionettes. It was so whimsical, it made her want to laugh when wooden Pamino ran from the jointed green puppet serpent, but somewhere between Sarastro's aria and Tamino and Pamina's trials, she had forgotten they were puppets and wept hearing Mozart's beautiful, solemn notes.

She told about the Englischer Garten, inspired by New York's Central Park, to be a country garden in the city, and how the beer gardens there were filled with the old folks—men and women—dressed neatly in their boiled wool jackets, drinking enormous steins of beer along with their Apfelkuchen. She paused briefly and with a faraway look in her eyes, recounted that everywhere there were so many fewer men than women. There were so many men dead in the war and so many widows left. There was a whole swath of society missing, mostly common foot soldiers doing the bidding of the madmen in Berlin. It was depressing. She thought about Heinrich, growing up with his father fighting far away as one of those foot soldiers on the eastern front, and then one day learning he wouldn't ever be coming home. He had never wanted to talk about it. What was there to say? How was his life any different from the thousands of others who'd lost fathers in the war?

Helen was quiet, thinking, and after a few moments she realized that the other two were waiting politely for her to continue. She smiled instead, unsure what to say next. Thomas gazed at her for a long moment, seeming to feel her unease.

"So," said Thomas breezily, sitting up. "I assume you speak German, then. Perhaps you'd be willing to tutor me a little? I've got an exam coming up next month, and my irregular verbs need help. That is, of course, if you have any spare time from The Committee."

"Oh, I suppose maybe I could find a little time," Helen said carelessly, "if I don't sprain anything else."

Chapter 4

On Monday morning, with Rose's help, Helen got out the door and back to the office. The prolonged weekend on the sofa had refreshed her, and she felt more than equal to the challenges of Mr. Major's demands, as well as to her own social ones. Ivan the Terrible came by her desk mid-morning—full of seriousness—to ask about her ankle and how she had injured it. He knitted his great dark brows together and nodded gravely. Then he held up his index finger to his lips and said, "My grandmother had a good pudding for such injuries."

Helen stared at him blankly.

"Pudding?" he tried again. "Perhaps this is not the correct word."

"Oh, really? I'm sure she did," replied Helen vaguely and without much concern. Over Ivan's shoulder she could see Vladimir making his way across the room toward her desk in front of Mr. Major's office. He carried a small bunch of purple asters, which she was sure were for her.

"Ahhh... *poultice*, I think is the word!" said Ivan after some thought. "It was a mustard poultice, very good for sprains."

Vladimir appeared at his elbow and smiled at Helen. "Ah yes, our old Russian grandmothers had many things we no longer want or need, didn't they?" He passed Helen the asters with a slight bow of his head and added, "You'd better heal up rapidly. We soon must dance the others off their feet, you know."

Ivan turned and looked hard at his rival, his brows so tight together that they formed a single dark line over his pale face, like a mink loping across a snow field. Then he turned again and looked hard at her for one very uncomfortable moment before he stumped off.

***

Helen quickly learned to maneuver on her crutches, and while she eschewed the subway for the following few weeks, she enjoyed the ease with which she obtained a seat on the morning commuter bus with her crutches in hand and her ankle brace. She had to plan more time to get to the office, but to have so many handsome men jump to her attention made it almost worth the trouble. Thomas Lawson had even showed up again once on her afternoon bus and walked her home. The pain in her ankle had subsided and kept at bay as long as she didn't put weight on it.

The one remaining problem was a dress. The Committee's Émigré Ball was now just over a month away. Helen had planned on wearing the one formal dress that she owned. She had purchased it in Munich for a fancy dress ball there—a strapless sheath, bias cut, with a sweetheart bodice and a skirt that narrowed down the legs. It was blue, a deep royal blue that Heinrich had said brought out her blue eyes, "like jewels." She recalled now, wryly, that it was one of the few poetic things he had ever said. On crutches and with her ankle in a brace, that dress with its narrowing skirt was out of the question. Rose offered her one of her own outfits, but Helen was just enough taller than petite Rose that anything of hers would be too small. Buying a new dress was out of the question. Since she had just arrived in the city, her income was already stretched from purchasing office attire and furnishings for the apartment. Yet, attending the ball in style was paramount.

The answer came that week in the mail. Heinrich had sent a birthday card, though early, for her birthday was not until October. With his letter, he enclosed a money order.

Dearest Helen,

I hope this letter finds you well-rested and happy for your 26th birthday. I trust that this year will bring us to some sort of reconciliation as this distance is too great and we cannot continue in this way. I know that you needed a respite from life here, but when you are rested I long for your return home. Enclosed is a gift for your birthday. I hope you will use it to buy something you like and find useful. Mutti sends her love. She misses having another woman in the family. Siegfried also sends his greeting. I send you all my love and my wishes for our future together.

Your loving husband, Heinrich

Helen opened the money order and sent a fleeting thought of gratitude to Heinrich. It would be enough for a dress. She thought of Siegfried, Heinrich's free-spirited younger brother, always laughing and concocting a new adventure. If only Heinrich had been more like that, things would have gone on better. She thought of Heinrich's mother and felt a pang of regret. Mutti had been so genuinely happy to have a daughter and had treated Helen like one, or even better, smilingly taking on the tedious tasks of ironing and cleaning that Helen couldn't stand. Helen knew Mutti would have done anything in her power to make Helen happy. But changing the way Heinrich was hadn't been in her power.

But she couldn't dwell on these thoughts right now. The problem of funds for the dress had cleared up; now she must make plans for obtaining one. The more Helen thought about how, and thought about the amount of the money order, the more her habitual thoughts of frugality slipped away. She decided she would treat herself to a well-made dress. It was what Heinrich would want her to have, something of quality, a new frock to celebrate her new life.

Helen shared her dilemma with Rose and, as always, her roommate came through and knew just what to do. Rose was fairly new to the city herself, and didn't know any dressmakers, but she knew someone who would. Rose's Great Aunt Martha had lived her entire maiden life in Manhattan and knew someone in nearly every neighborhood and every profession. When Rose called her up, Helen could hear the old woman's voice through the telephone receiver from clear across the room. Her voice was boisterous and lively, but not very ladylike.

"You need to go see Clementine," boomed Aunt Martha, saying the name with a French pronunciation, Clemen-*teen*. "She's not far from you girls, on 82nd. She's a darn good seamstress, though Lord knows I haven't had anything made for me in awhile, probably not since the last of my friends was married off, and that's been a few years, I can tell you! Ha! Old maiden aunts don't have much call for fancy new frills."

Helen covered her mouth to muffle her laugh while she listened to the verbal barrage emitted from the receiver. Rose held the telephone a few inches from her ear, and smiled at Helen but listened attentively to her aunt, uttering an "uh-huh" and "oh" when she could.

"Anyway, go see Clementine," continued Aunt Martha. "Clementine Cavaziel, she'll be in the book. You'll like her, she's foreign. She worked for the Higgins family for years and years and years. You know, Louise Higgins, who I went to school with. Or rather, 'with whom I went to school' I'd better say before Miss Schoolteacher corrects my grammar. Anyway, that's what you should do. Well, nice to talk to you, dear, but I'm off to poker now. Goodbye."

When Rose had said a mild "goodbye" to her aunt who had already hung up, she turned to Helen.

"Aunt Martha is the character of the family. She's my Grandma Elizabeth's younger sister. She's loyal as a mother bobcat, but you mustn't interfere with her poker game and you mustn't expect to get a word in edgewise."

Chapter 5

The following Wednesday, Helen slipped out from work an hour early, and at four-thirty found herself on East 82nd Street in front of the neat, four-story apartment building where Miss Clementine Cavaziel lived. There was no elevator, and Helen progressed slowly up the stairs, gripping the railing with one hand and her crutches with the other. By the time she reached the third floor, she was feeling hot and annoyed. A door on the landing was opened by a skinny older woman. She was buttoning up a long black raincoat, and with her dark hair swept up into a tight bun at the very crown of her head, she looked like an inverted exclamation point. She looked at Helen and her eyes registered a parallel surprise.

"Miss Cavaziel?" Helen asked.

"Upstairs, dear, on the opposite side," the woman said, pointing to the ceiling with a bony index finger. Helen fumbled on, and when she finally reached the landing on the fourth floor, she was feeling that this much trouble for a new dress was a faulty idea. But before she had time to dwell on the fact, the door opened and there stood Miss Cavaziel.

She looked younger than she had sounded on the telephone, but Helen realized that her accent had made it difficult to judge. She was in her early fifties. Curly auburn hair fringed above her tortoise shell glasses, which in turn framed bright, inquisitive green eyes. She held out her hand, and as she shook Helen's gloved one, she pulled her firmly through the doorway, crutches and all.

"Come in, come in, pleased to meet you," she said as she took Helen's coat and then led her down the hallway. "You said on the telephone that Martha Smith gave you my name. How is she nowadays? I don't believe I've seen her since I worked for Mrs. Higgins, but it's very thoughtful of her to send you to me."

Her English was flawless, but she had a strong accent that Helen could not place. It sounded Germanic, but not quite German, at least not like the German accents she had heard in Munich. She led Helen to a sitting room on the right. There was one large window that let in the afternoon light. It was sparsely but tastefully furnished and tidily kept. There was a large bookcase and a coffee table made of warm honey-colored wood, and two red cushions brightened the otherwise plain brown sofa. A large painting of a mountain landscape hung over the sofa, and, at Miss Cavaziel's invitation, Helen sat in one of two green plush armchairs that flanked the bookcase and faced the sofa and the painting.

"Let me take your things, then we can talk a bit about what style you would like before I take your measurements," said Miss Cavaziel in a friendly tone. "I'm sorry that you have hurt yourself. What has happened to you?"

With a sigh, Helen explained about the sprain, the ankle brace, and her need for a new dress for the ball.

"I just hope, Miss Cavaziel, that three weeks will be enough time."

"Oh, I think we can manage it. You are fortunate in that most of the autumn season society dresses have already been made, and the wedding season is now behind us. I think we will do fine. Only one thing I insist," and she looked at Helen sharply, "you must call me Clementine. Miss Clementine, if you must. But leave off the Cavaziel. It's a beautiful name, but difficult to spell and horrible for Americans to pronounce. Calling by first names is an American habit that I've grown to like."

As she spoke, she brought two large volumes of fashion design books from the bookcase and set them on the coffee table in front of Helen. A faint chime sounded as a clock on the side table announced it was quarter-to-five.

"You look through those for inspiration, and I'll just go to make coffee," said Clementine. *Miss* Clementine, insisted Helen to herself, who did not like to break with tradition unless it was her own idea.

When Clementine returned with coffee a few minutes later, Helen sat with a book on her knees. As she looked through the full-color plates, she stopped at a page showing a full-skirted princess waist dress with a fitted bodice. Clementine set the coffee and cups on the table and looked over Helen's shoulder.

"Ah, yessss..." She backed up and sized Helen up. "Do you like that one? Because I think it will suit you nicely, and do well with the circumstances. We could add cap sleeves to make walking with the crutches easier." She sat on the sofa across from Helen, poured a cup of coffee, and asked as she passed it across the table to her, "Will you take a coffee?"

As it seemed too late to decline, Helen answered politely, "Yes please, thank you," although it seemed more of a cocktail time of day. From a drawer in the table, Clementine pulled out a small package of chocolates and set them in between them. She then poured her own cup, added milk and sugar, and sat back on the sofa.

"I always have coffee at this time of day. It's an old habit from home." Helen, burning to know where her home was, nonchalantly took a large sip of her coffee and tried not to seem too curious. The coffee was strong and hot and burned the top of her tongue. Self-consciously, she added more milk and took another sip. Whether or not she could sense Helen's curiosity, Clementine continued,

"I am from Switzerland. I came to the United States in my early twenties and have been working here since then."

Ah, Switzerland. That explained the accent as well as the chocolates.

"It's a beautiful country!" said Helen. "I went there on my...trip." She had been about to say "honeymoon", but stopped herself.

"Oh, you have been to Switzerland? Most people who say Switzerland is beautiful have never been there, and I always wonder that its reputation can have spread so far."

"Yes, I...we...when I lived in Munich I went to Lucerne for a few days. We took the boat on the Vierwaldstätter See, and the train up the Rigi. It was breathtaking." Fleeting memories of that trip went through her mind, how sweet Heinrich had been, how happy they had been together. How she had twisted her ankle badly then, too, hiking down the Rigi, and how tenderly and patiently Heinrich had cared for her.

"So you lived in Munich?" asked Clementine with interest. "Do you speak German?"

"Ein bisschen," *A little*, Helen replied, pleased to display her German to someone in New York. "Wie geht es Ihnen?" *How are you?*

Clementine smiled. "Es gaht mir guet!" "I think my Swiss German sounds a little different to you, doesn't it? Most Germans don't understand it very well, even the ones from southern Germany."

The two women smiled at each other as they sipped, and a sense of camaraderie filled the room with the aroma of the strong coffee as they talked about places that were far away and yet familiar to both of them.

"Don't you miss it? Your home, I mean," asked Helen suddenly.

"Yes, I do miss home. I miss my family. But people there have their own problems, just like people here." She sighed and set down her empty cup. "And my home is here now."

Chapter 6

The following week Mr. Major was away in Washington, D.C. for two days, so Helen left work early on Thursday afternoon to see Clementine again and choose her dress fabric. Thomas Lawson was coming over in the early evening for the first German tutoring session, but there was time beforehand. She took the bus up Lexington Avenue and arrived at 3:30. It was a drizzly grey afternoon, and while the maples had begun to turn glowing shades of red and yellow, they were dripping with rain. Helen was getting adept at using her crutches, but they made it impossible to hold an umbrella, and the two-block walk from the bus had dampened not only her spirits, but the rest of her as well. Clementine had apparently just returned from errands herself. A dripping umbrella stood like a guard on the landing outside her door, and when she opened it, her spectacles were still foggy from condensation. But she smiled warmly and helped Helen off with her soggy coat. A bag of groceries waited outside the door to the tiny kitchen, and next to a stack of mail on the hall table stood a tiny goat carved out of wood. The letters in the stack of mail were slightly askew and therefore, looked out of place in the orderly apartment. Helen didn't mean to snoop, but her eye caught the top-most letter. It was addressed in the large careful hand of a schoolgirl and bore a Swiss stamp.

Though Helen had only visited once before, Clementine's apartment felt familiar and comfortable on this rainy afternoon, as if the walls and furniture understood the connection Helen already felt to their owner. Helen was grateful to sink into the green chair in the calmness of that sitting room, and gaze at the mountain scene on the wall. So far, the work week had been a trying one, even with Mr. Major out of the way for a few days, and she was glad of something else to occupy her thoughts. She looked forward to chatting more with Clementine. She seemed like the kind of person she could really talk to, who had traveled and was a career woman. But this time Clementine seemed disinclined to converse. She was businesslike, and as soon as Helen was seated she bustled off to find the fabric samples she had to show her.

"We should be able to choose quickly enough," Clementine said briskly as she sat opposite Helen. She opened her folder and spread swatches of fabrics on the table. The bright orange and yellow hues that were so popular this year jumbled together with more muted tones of blue, green, and amethyst. Clementine worked quickly through the selections, muttering as she went. There were so many colors and sorts of fabric, all suited for an evening dress. One by one she held them up next to Helen's face.

"Not black, I think. Classic, but too stark with your fair complexion. Navy is better, but still almost harsh. Red would be amusing, if we could find the right shade. No, no, no," as she held up a scarlet swatch. Then a burgundy taffeta. "Not quite right for the season. No, I don't think red is for you."

On and on she went, and Helen, wondering if she should offer an opinion, realized that she didn't really have one and was happy to let Clementine carry on and find something flattering. Finally she came to a dead stop. "Yes. This one!" she said firmly, and Helen—who hadn't really paid attention the last few seconds—looked down to her shoulder to find a swatch of rich emerald sateen.

"Really? Are you sure? I never wear much green." She hadn't, in fact, since the second grade. She'd gotten a new green dress for her birthday and been so proud to wear it to school, until Mary Finnigan had said she looked like a leprechaun. And Mary would have known; she was Irish.

"Yes. I am sure. A dramatic color, but not harsh and not garish. It will be lovely on you." She said this with such a note of finality that since Helen hadn't had much to say before, she didn't feel like she could argue much now. Clementine brought her a hand mirror, and she had to admit that it was a nice shade. She had always had a nice complexion, and somehow the color brought out its fair creaminess. Perhaps it was time to leave the second grade behind her.

"Well then, good, that's done," said Clementine as she picked up the other fabric squares. "I will begin this week, and you should come back in two weeks to fit it."

She seemed distracted, and Helen knew it would be good manners to leave now, but she didn't want to go. She liked it here. To be honest, she had been looking forward to another conversation with Clementine. What could she say to draw her out? Her eye moved to the painting on the opposite wall.

"It's a lovely painting. Is that somewhere in Switzerland?"

She had chosen the right topic. Clementine looked up at it, then straightened up, adjusted her glasses, and cocked her head thoughtfully to one side.

"That is my mountain, the Tödi," she said softly. "My younger brother painted it. He is an artist. It is the mountain above our village where we would take our cows to the Alp in summer."

Helen was enchanted. She wanted to hear more. The chime on the clock sounded.

Clementine visibly relaxed, and then cocked her head to one side again and looked straight at Helen.

"I will make us some coffee, alright?"

Over their hot coffee, Clementine told an eager Helen about her village in the Alpine valley where the great and mighty Rhine River began as just a small stream. Helen learned that Clementine's native language was not Swiss German after all, but Romantsch. It was the descendant of the Latin brought by the Romans in ancient times as they went about conquering everything. The mountain valleys were so remote that after the Romans settled down, people mostly stayed put, and there was only the occasional visit from traders and travelers who would brave the mountain passes in the warm summer months when the snow pack was passable. With their metal trinkets and other wares, they brought news of the world beyond the Alpine walls of granite and when they moved on, they left behind new Germanic words that were slowly accepted into the local vernacular.

"It's a dying language though," Clementine said matter-of-factly. "There are only 40,000 of us left who speak it, and many of those leave the valleys, marry elsewhere, and speak to their children in their new language."

"Oh, what a pity!" cried Helen.

"Yes, it is. But I cannot blame anyone; I went away, too." She paused thoughtfully. "There are some people who have started a movement to defend our language and teach it in the schools. It is a good thing, but perhaps too late."

Helen was sad and felt silly for feeling so, since she had learned of the existence of the language not even ten minutes ago.

"What is it like, your language?" she asked.

Clementine got up, crossed the room to the bookshelf behind Helen, and pulled down a small black volume. La Biblia was engraved in gold letters across the front. She opened it and held it so Helen could read along above where her finger was pointing.

All 'entschatta era il Vierv, ed il Vierv era tier Diu, e Dieu sera il Vierv.

After she had read, Clementine slowly translated the words into English.

In the beginning was the Word, and the Word was with God and the Word was God.

The language sounded more different than anything Helen had heard before. On the page she could see a resemblance to the little she knew of Italian, but the words that Clementine was reading had a sing-song cadence and harder consonant tones, like those of German. Clementine flipped a few pages, poked her finger down, and read again.

Pilver, pilver, jeu ditgel a vus: Sch'il semsalin croda buc et tratsch e miera, resta el persuls; mo sch'el miera, porta el bia tretg.

Truly, truly I say to you, unless a grain of wheat falls into the earth and dies, it remains alone; but if it dies, it bears much fruit.

Clementine looked at Helen and smiled shyly. "It feels so strange to hear these words out loud. I don't speak Romantsch much these days. When I first got here, I knew a girl from Chur who worked in a bakery in Greenwich Village. We would meet and speak our language, but we lost touch eventually."

As she closed the Bible, the chime rang five o'clock. It seemed to Helen that a sweet spell had been broken, just like in the fairy tales, and to her surprise she was still in New York and it was time to go home.

Chapter 7

The next two weeks were terribly busy at work. During the third week of October, students in Hungary marched through Budapest, demanding free elections and withdrawal of the Soviet army. In the streets they broadcasted Radio Free Europe from loudspeakers on the top of a van, and more demonstrators joined them until the country came to a standstill and the world watched. News of what was happening on the ground became essential, not only for the outside world, but for the Hungarians themselves, and The Committee's offices in New York hummed with purpose.

Even so, Helen was not so busy that she didn't have time to go out for cocktails with Vladimir when he asked. Now that he had secured her as a date for the Émigré Ball, he seemed intent on securing all her other attentions as well. He was absolutely charming, holding the doors, always helping her on with her coat, and though she tried to appear aloof, Helen drank up his attentions like a sponge. He was so well-traveled! And well-spoken! In several languages! And surely—said a nagging little voice in her mind, he was the kind of worldly experienced man who would understand her particular...situation, and wouldn't be put off by the prospect of a divorcée. Not that that's what she was yet, technically, but she would be soon enough when it was all arranged. And in the meantime, she hoped he wouldn't mind too much that her affairs weren't completely in order.

Friday evening Vladimir had taken her to the China House for dinner, and afterward he escorted her home and met Rose. The three of them shared a nightcap in their living room, Rose curled up in the big green armchair, and she and Vladimir on the blue sofa, separated by a distance big enough to be appropriate, but close enough to be meaningful. *The Winter's Tale*, which Rose had been reading for school when they arrived, lay on the side table next to her. She gazed at them amiably and smiled politely at Vladimir's charming conversation.

The look on Rose's face reminded Helen of the day she had brought Roger Brown home for her mother's inspection before the Junior Class dance. Her mother had been reading Shakespeare, too, had laid down her book, and waited politely while Roger stammered out a few awkward sentences. He had passed muster. He had taken her to the dance and then became almost otherwise completely forgettable. A nice enough face, Helen had thought to herself at the time, but just not too much going on upstairs. And quite a bore. All she ever needed or wanted to know about bowling leagues she had already heard from her father and didn't need Roger's perspective.

What an entirely different experience with Vladimir. Yet she couldn't shake the feeling that Rose was just wishing to be back in her book. After he had left Helen on her doorstep with a warm kiss lingering on her cheek, she swooned back into the living room and flopped onto the couch.

"Isn't he dreamy?" Helen asked breathlessly. Her nerves were still standing on end, crackling from being near him. Rose's eyes met hers with brows raised in question. From her hand dangled the book that she had picked up again. She tapped it against her knee.

"Well...he isn't *my* type."

Helen sat up. "What do you mean?"

"Hmmm...well, since you ask, if you don't mind my saying so, even though he is your date, he seems rather full of himself."

"No, he isn't!" Helen hotly protested. "He's just confident! And he's so considerate toward me!"

She thought for a minute about the conversation they had just had. Vladimir had been telling them about the dances he had been to as a child in Paris amid the large Russian émigré community. Once, his grandmother had burst into tears because, though the balls were wonderful and still boasted attendance by most of the old Russian aristocracy, their grandeur was nothing in comparison to the balls she had known before, when even the czar and his family would attend.

Then he had spoken of his years in boarding school in London during the war, the connections he had made there, and how his family was still one of the best connected among Europe's new postwar governing elite. Helen had found it all incredibly riveting, but she did have to admit, in retrospect, that while seeming to want to gain Rose's approval, he hadn't found the time to ask her anything meaningful about her own life. Well, she thought reasonably, I suppose I already told him she was a schoolteacher. Maybe he couldn't think of anything else to ask.

"Well," said Rose finally, to Helen who was lost in her own thoughts, "At least I'm sure he'll be a good dancer."

***

The next Wednesday afternoon, Mr. Major flew down to Washington to meet with the Hungarian delegation. Helen was grateful for the respite from his constant, ever-changing demands and was spending a quiet afternoon catching up on his correspondence. Sitting at her desk, she leaned forward again to smell the small bouquet of yellow and pink roses Vladimir had brought by her desk Monday morning. The yellow ones smelled the strongest, of a spicy tea. She inhaled deeply, closing her eyes. From the far end of the room, she heard Vladimir's voice. She felt the butterflies in her stomach flutter as, across the bank of secretaries' desks, she heard him greeting Elaine and Pansy in passing. She glanced up quickly in his direction. He was listening to Elaine, but intrinsically she felt that everything but his gaze was directed at her. It was a game they were playing, she thought, as she took another peek and saw him stopped at Lily's desk. He was advancing slowly, like a snow leopard, across the room toward her. She did her best to appear intently engaged in her work, not paying him any mind. She put another piece of paper in the typewriter and began the memo to the Munich office. Her scribbled notes lay across her desk, but she couldn't focus on the transcription. When he was halfway across the room, moving ever steadily in her direction in his slow elegant saunter, she ventured a peek and found him staring straight at her, the expression in his pale blue eyes serious, but a smile playing around his lips. She caught her breath and quickly bent her head to finish the memo.

She felt Vladimir glide into her presence. Nonchalantly, he placed himself on the corner of her desk. She slowly breathed in the scent of his aftershave, musky and expensive.

"Your hair, it is very lovely today, Helen, the way you've pinned it back on that side."

She flushed, surprised but gratified that he would notice and say something about her hair. Of course, she had thought of him this morning, when she pinned it back, hoping that he would notice. With effort, she willed herself to be as nonchalant as he was and looked up at him. His gaze startled her. Steady, steely, and clear, it communicated possession. She felt disoriented, thrilled, annoyed, and a little frightened. She felt her cheeks turning pinker and heard her voice mumble, "Thank you." His steady pale blue eyes moved over her hair to her face and then down, taking in the curves of her body appreciatively.

"Ah-em!" she cleared her throat and became very businesslike. She slammed the arm of the typewriter across and advanced the paper. The memo continued... *avoid to the utmost extent any explicit or implicit support of individual personalities in a temporary government – especially of communist personalities such as ....blah, blah, blah...* It was impossible to think about the words, with him sitting there staring at her like that. She wondered what the other secretaries were thinking.

"You are very busy, I see. I really don't want to bother you," said Vladimir in a voice that implied he was very happy doing just that. "Mr. Major and his unending memos." He paused. "Where is this one to?"

Helen was glad to keep the conversation on work. "To the Munich office. There have been a lot these days, you know, with what's going on in Hungary."

"Ah, yes, they have kept me at the translation desk with the news reports. But it's not so very interesting, for me, you know, when I have so many other skills." He practically whispered it.

"Yes, I am *sure* you do," said Helen coquettishly with a glance up at him. She sat up in her chair a bit, trying to regain her businesslike composure. "All the same, what you do *is* terribly important. Just like me typing this memo," she added officiously.

With that, Vladimir stood up with a sigh and a smile. "I know when I am being dismissed. Back to my desk." He started to walk off. Helen was almost disappointed; then Vladimir turned, eyeing her once again with his forceful gaze. "For Saturday... I'll come at seven."

The rest of that afternoon, Helen felt discomfited, but was unsure why. She told herself that she should feel flattered that Vladimir found her physically attractive. She had the Emigré Ball to look forward to, a beautiful new dress, and the prospect of an enticing relationship with a very interesting man. A man—she was reassured to remember—who hadn't seemed to mind what she'd told him about Heinrich on their last date. That was something.

***

The next day she went to Clementine's to pick up her dress. Helen was not a person given to false modesty, and when she admired herself in the full-length mirror to which Clementine took her, she could only agree with the petite seamstress. It was stunning. *She* was stunning. Clementine was also very pleased.

"Yes, yes," Clementine said, in a self-congratulatory tone. This is what I imagined. Didn't you imagine it, too?"

Helen just beamed. She hadn't particularly imagined anything, but she was immensely happy with the result, and couldn't wait for Vladimir to see her on Saturday night. She had moved beyond her crutches now, and could walk with only the brace. It would almost not show, and she was sure she'd be up for a few dances as well. It was all splendid and exactly what she wanted.

Chapter 8

The much-anticipated Saturday came soon enough. But when she awoke that morning, Helen lay in bed awhile, considering the thought that had buzzed around her mind like a fly for some time and had now finally alighted on her shoulder: what would she look forward to tomorrow? She got up, dressed, and puttered around the apartment for a while. The weather was overcast and gray, but neither warm nor cold, as if it couldn't decide whether to hearken back to the early days of autumn or to press on determinedly toward winter. The apartment seemed warm and stuffy, but on the terrace outside it was too cold. Just when Helen had begun thinking about making preparations to do her hair, the doorbell rang. Helen quickly thought of Vladimir. He was certainly the type to have a corsage delivered. But when Rose went to answer the door, to Helen's surprise it was Thomas Lawson. His attempt at arranging German lessons had been lost in her autumn activities, and she hadn't seen him since the last time they'd rode the bus together. He invited her for coffee at the café down the street. Helen had plenty to do to get ready for the evening, but it was still early, and he seemed so bright and eager that she felt she would be callous to turn him down. As they walked along the sidewalk and over the crosswalk, they laughed together about their first painful walk from the bus stop only a few weeks ago.

"I was in your neighborhood and thought I'd drop by and see how your ankle is doing. And see how the liberation from communism is going. The Hungarians seem to be liberating themselves."

"Don't make fun!" Helen pretended to be indignant. Then she changed her tone to one that she hoped sounded mysterious. "Our work is *very* important, and yes, we *are* part of the Hungarian effort. Well, at least, the European desk is. My work is mostly with the Russian broadcasts."

They sat in the café with their coffee, and with a note of self-importance she told him about the Émigré Ball she was attending that very evening and the crowd of illustrious freedom agitators who were sure to be there. And with seeming indifference, she told him about her date, Vladimir Demidoff, and his interesting life and many accomplishments. For a moment, she wished that Thomas could see her in her beautiful new gown as well. Then she laughed to herself. Why did she care what he thought of her? He was so odd. Even now, he sat there running his fingers through his already wild hair, his wrinkled mustard-colored jacket clashing mightily with the green shirt he wore underneath it. She noticed, now, that his grey eyes had a kind of faraway look as she chattered on about Vladimir. Suddenly, his expression changed. He was growing unsettled. It was like watching a storm cloud approaching and finding herself without an umbrella.

"He's probably a spy!" Thomas spat out in total earnestness. "He's just using you to get information!"

Helen was flabbergasted.

"Thomas, don't be silly! He's from a very respectable family who had to flee the Revolution! And anyway, what kind of information could *I* give him? I don't do anything very important."

"No? I thought you told me it was extremely important. I thought you were personally saving the world from communism."

"Oh, you know what I mean. Anyway, that's the most ludicrous thing I've ever heard; you've read too many spy novels."

Thomas forced a chuckle, but his ruddy cheeks turned a deeper shade, and Helen knew that her last statement had hit truth.

"All the same, be careful; in the books it's always those suave, multilingual characters who are trouble."

When Thomas walked Helen back to the door of her apartment, Rose was just returning from Saturday morning errands. She came out of the elevator, her arms full of packages. Thomas reached to help her, and Helen noticed that she greeted Thomas with a genuine smile that she hadn't graced upon Vladimir. When Thomas had taken his leave, Rose turned to Helen.

"There! He's the sort of man you ought to spend more time with." She said it decidedly, a fixed light in her eyes. "He's thoughtful, authentic, and he respects you."

"I had just been thinking that he would be a good match for you, dear Rose," replied Helen, "and I guess he would be if you admire him that much."

Rose's laughter cascaded like a mountain brook. "No, not *me*! It's not me he's interested in. Honestly, Helen, do you think you sprained your eyes along with your ankle?"

This gave Helen pause. Was she missing something? She remembered Thomas' moment in the café, his moment of anger...*jealousy*? Really? Thomas was certainly a nice, albeit odd, young man, but she'd never intentionally given him reason to admire her. He was not at all the kind of man that she found attractive. Well, she was sorry, she thought ruefully, if it meant hurting his feelings one day. Heaven knew, she was getting practiced at that. Her mind flew quickly to Heinrich, but she forced it to turn away. Tonight was the ball that she had been looking forward to for weeks, and she would not let anything steal her enjoyment of that.

Chapter 9

In the taxi headed down 5th Avenue, Helen wanted to pinch herself. She was in New York City, headed to a society event at the Waldorf Astoria Hotel. She knew she looked beautiful, and knowing it gave her the confidence that made her even more so. When he'd picked her up, for a moment even Vladimir the Debonair had looked stunned. For just an instant, she'd seen his guard down, and he'd been speechless. Just a murmur of "absolutely beautiful" passed his lips as he'd helped her on with her coat. She'd felt triumphant as he'd helped her into the cab. But as they neared their destination, the feeling faded. Vladimir had been attentive to her and exchanged pleasantries with the driver, but now he seemed increasingly distracted and lost in his own thoughts. He hunched into his side of the cab, the lapels on his tuxedo bunched up askew. Helen wondered what she had done.

"Are you...are you feeling alright, Vladimir?" she ventured.

"Of course I am!" he spat out. Then he shook his head quickly and added, "I'm sorry, darling. I'm tired from these damn long workdays. I'll be fine when I've had a drink." He flashed her a quick smile and then reached out and put his hand on her knee. Then he turned and stared moodily out the window at the lights of the buildings passing by on the Avenue. Helen pulled her knee away and stared out the window on her side.

Once inside the glittering ballroom, the thoughts of their awkward taxi ride fled. The room was filling rapidly with groups of the most elegant ladies and gentlemen Helen had ever laid eyes on. She heard different languages on every side, saw gentlemen bowing, and older women wearing finely cut jewels in their hair and around their necks. It was like falling into a novel. The allure of Old World sophistication in the room intoxicated Helen. Even before the waiters had served them long stems of champagne, Vladimir had shed his moodiness and stood straight and tall in his perfectly fitted set of tails. He was completely at home in this milieu and apparently knew most of the people in the room. Slowly they strolled around the grand ballroom, arm in arm, as he introduced Helen to several choice specimens: a count here, a duchess there, here the Countess who had been at boarding school in Paris with his grandmother before the Revolution. He glided like a dancer from one conversation to the next, moving with as much ease from one language to another—French, German, or Russian, as the situation required. Helen earnestly wished she had continued the Russian lessons she had begun in Munich so she could understand more. During a brief lull in conversation, Vladimir turned his pale gaze on her and smiled wryly. The fatigue of the taxi ride had vanished, and he seemed to be enjoying her obvious pleasure at mixing with high Russian society. He made up for her lack of title by introducing her as the Exceedingly Charming Helen Hartmann. Helen's cheeks grew hot with self-consciousness, but the exquisite old ladies to whom she was introduced obliged her to feel at ease with their gracious smiles and the pressure of their hands, each enveloped in elbow-length white kid gloves. It was divine. One beautiful old countess—her shining silver hair swept up in a tower on her head and adorned with a diamond tiara—continued smiling kindly at Helen while she spoke, at length, to Vladimir in Russian. She glanced at him and then back at Helen, raising her eyebrows meaningfully. Vladimir answered the woman in a tone that sounded self-effacing, but he flashed Helen such an engaging smile that she felt her cheeks grow warmer yet.

That was the nicest part of the evening.

When the Countess had turned smilingly away, in front of them materialized a short man in a pin-striped suit. He was about Helen's age, but his dark hair had a white streak that swooped up from his widow's peak, thick with hair ointment. On his arm was a very thin, very fair woman with cold blue eyes in a blue dress to match.

"Ah, Boris!" Vladimir exclaimed. "I wasn't sure you would be here."

"But I am, Vladimir, as you can see." He stood staring at Vladimir through an awkward pause. "You remember my sister, Natasha." He nodded at the lady to his side without taking his gaze off of Vladimir. The latter inclined his head politely.

"And this is Helen Hartmann," he answered simply, with a quick glance at her. His smile was gone.

"We must talk," said Boris heavily.

What a rude man, Helen thought.

The two men stared at each other a long moment. Vladimir turned to Helen.

"Listen, Helen darling, Boris and I have got a little business to attend to. I'm so sorry. It won't be more than a few minutes. Wait for me here, won't you?"

Helen felt nervous, so she drew herself up and tried to look haughty. She exhaled loudly and muttered, "Oh, of course. I'll wait for you here."

She smiled with what she hoped looked like self-confidence and raised her glass of champagne to her lips as she watched the two men retreating to the corner of the room.

***

Two and a half hours later, Helen sat up in her chair. She imagined herself as a patient person, but this was scandalous. Vladimir had yet to resurface, and by now she was exceedingly annoyed. Natasha, the icy stick woman, had remained rigidly by her side for the first half hour. Her presence made Helen feel extremely uncomfortable. She stood too close. Helen stepped a little farther to one side and glanced around the room. The glittering society continued around her as before, but it had lost its enchantment to her.

"So," she ventured to the woman next to her, "you have only just arrived from somewhere?"

"Yes. We live in Paris," the woman said with finality. Then she said no more, and a few minutes later she walked away without taking her leave.

Helen saw Vladimir at one point, about three quarters of an hour after he had left, up in one of the boxes overlooking the ballroom. Now there were two other men with Boris and the four of them appeared to be in a heated discussion. Helen watched for a while, and when she caught his eye as he glanced down, he flashed her an apologetic smile, raising a finger as if to say that they were almost finished, and then turned back to the debate. About that time, the buffet dinner service began. After waiting another quarter hour out of politesse, Helen got up and helped herself. She was famished and frustrated.

When the dancing began, Helen did her best to appear as though she liked nothing better than sitting alone and watching. The dancers were beautiful. Back and forth across the polished floor they glided in the most intricate patterns, weaving the tapestry of tradition with each precise step of their feet. Each couple was absolutely absorbed in themselves and, at the same time, aware of all the others. These were people who had grown up on the ballroom floor, each learning his or her role from a tender age. Helen consoled herself with the thought that she would not have to feel out of place out there. She was a decent dancer herself, but nothing compared to this. Of course, she mused, Vladimir would have made up for that. He, too, had been born to this life, and would have led her through a waltz with grace and ease. The thought upset her again. She became aware of a small knot of women nearby speaking rapidly in

Russian. The silver-haired Countess was murmuring excitedly to a few other elegant women, nodding occasionally at Helen with a look of pity on her refined face. Helen's cheeks flushed again, but this time from embarrassment and indignation.

Helen turned away and saw Ivan the Terrible approaching across the room, leading a young mousy girl. Too late, Helen looked down, and Ivan's eye caught hers. She couldn't escape them. The mousy girl turned out to be his cousin, Svetlana, when he introduced her. He asked politely after Vladimir, and she stumbled over her words as she made an excuse for him. It was ridiculous. Why should she have to make excuses for him? Ivan nodded and then knit his dark brows together. Then he gazed at her a long moment, looking almost sorry for her. It unnerved Helen, and she rose and excused herself. Ivan led his young cousin onto the dance floor.

She was upset enough that a little later, when two different gentlemen asked for the pleasure of a dance, she turned them down flat. She hadn't wanted to be pitied, and she no longer cared if she were thought rude. Now, after two hours, she was wishing a little that she hadn't been so stubborn. A dance or two with a polite and handsome stranger would have made her feel that the evening wasn't a complete waste of a beautiful, custom-tailored dress. She sighed. The first guests were beginning to leave, and it dawned on Helen that she might need to figure out for herself how to get home. She suddenly felt exhausted, and the thought of a carriage shrinking back into a pumpkin sprung to her mind. The reappearance of Natasha at her side brought her back to reality.

"Vladimir says to tell you that he is terribly, terribly sorry that he has been detained." Her tone was meant to convey sorrow, but the sad smile she conjured up for Helen mocked her with its insincerity.

"Oh," replied Helen. "Well, yes, I should certainly hope he is sorry." She tried desperately to sound more angry than flustered. "Won't he be coming soon?"

"He asked me to convey his deepest apologies and to give you this for your taxi ride home." She slipped a folded bill into Helen's hand.

"What?! No! I will not accept this!" she stammered. Though she tried to maintain the façade of Vladimir's accommodating and poised date, the evening had left her hurt, tired, and confused. Her better judgment was gone. A few heads turned as Helen asserted, "*He* should take me home! It's the least he can do!" She thrust the money back at Natasha, but she had already started walking away, saying airily, "Goodnight, Mrs. Hartmann."

Helen was stunned. She looked at the bill in her hand. It was fifty dollars, enough to take her home at least three times. Why had Vladimir given her so much money? How could he just leave her here like this? She felt cheap, as if she were being paid for her services. In the corners of her eyes, hot tears were welling. With difficulty, she blinked them away, and strode out of the shining ballroom and into the night as quickly as her ankle would allow.

Chapter 10

The crimson roses that arrived at her apartment the next day signed 'Vladimir' softened Helen's feelings ever so slightly, but there was no phone call, no explanation. The headache that had begun in the wee hours of a night of fitful sleep blossomed into a full migraine by early afternoon, and Helen went back to bed for the rest of the day with an eye shade and an ice pack.

***

On Monday the office was a tumult, like a beehive overturned by a grizzly bear. On Sunday, Soviet troops had marched into Budapest to crush the newborn Hungarian revolution, and the world was in shock. Typewriters clattered like mad, filling the room with a mechanical drone. There were memos to type and send to all the field offices, coordinating protocol in the face of such an affront to freedom. There was no sign of Vladimir, and even if there had been, Helen had no time to talk; Mr. Major kept Helen busy all day taking shorthand memos to send to Munich, to Washington, and to agents in undisclosed locations. She would have found the international tension terribly thrilling if her own feelings hadn't been so jumbled. Should she be upset with Vladimir for how she'd been treated? Or, she wondered, should she feel sorry for him that he'd gotten involved in some sort of troubling business? Mostly Helen felt simply exhausted, and back home that evening, after Rose had quietly listened to her ramble on about it for over an hour, she got up to go to bed.

"Dear Rose, what would I do without you? Thank you for listening to it all."

Rose stopped counting the stitches on the green striped scarf she was knitting, and looked up, surprised.

"Oh, Helen, of course. I suppose maybe someday you'll have to do the same for me." She smiled. "Goodnight."

Helen doubted it. She could hardly imagine gentle Rose needing to vent her feelings like she had done so often lately. Rose's influence was calming and peaceful instead. Helen felt grateful again that they had found each other.

***

Helen slept well and made her way into work the next morning feeling well-rested. An aura of Rose's tranquility from the night before still lingered. Then her peace dissolved.

"Did you hear it?" screeched Pansy the second Helen walked in the door of The Committee offices.

"Hear what?" asked Helen.

"He's gone! He was a *spy*!"

"Who? Pansy, who are you talking about? Calm down!"

"Calm down?! Calm *down*?! You won't be able to calm down when you hear all about it!" Pansy smacked her gum quickly, as if to gain strength. *"Vladimir Demidoff!* All this time, a spy for the Reds! I just dunno what to think!"

Neither did Helen. Everything was suddenly quiet and seemed to fade away. She stood, stunned, in front of Pansy's desk, trying to process what she'd just heard.

"But..I...What..." She couldn't seem to form a coherent question.

Pansy spewed out the answers like a cat drunk on a new ball of catnip. "Apparently someone waaay up," she raised her eyebrows mysteriously and looked toward the ceiling, "has suspected a mole here for a while, and then there was some sort of confrontation at the Émigré Ball. I figured you could tell me all about that! And then one of our fellas," she paused, putting on an enigmatic look, "looked a little closer at some of the private cables he was sending out. He was letting the Ruskies know just how committed we are to Eastern Europe. And this Hungarian thing brought it all to a head. Not just translating the weather forecast!"

"Oh my..." Helen started and trailed off in confusion.

"*Oh my* is right! I'll say! Oh my goodness and oh my stars and oh my God knows what else! And the Suez Canal thing on top of it all! By the way, Mary and I are going to the rally tomorrow night at Madison Square Garden protesting the Soviet invasion. Do ya wanna come along?"

It sounded like an invitation to a bridge party. Did she want to come along? No! She wanted to go somewhere quiet and carefully place her head under a rock.

"Yes...yes, of course. We must *do* something!" Helen's voice came out in a squeak. She was dying to ask what had become of Vladimir now, but she wouldn't dare ask. She didn't trust her voice to speak of him. A spy? What kind of strange story was she in? She unpacked her things at her desk, tuning out Pansy who had now begun to chatter about her lunch plans. Helen tried to focus her thoughts by arranging things and looking over the memos from yesterday that she needed to type for Mr. Major. He was out of his office, Pansy had said, upstairs in an emergency meeting.

As Helen began typing the first memo to the Munich office, her stomach lurched. She thought of Vladimir's afternoon visits in the past few weeks, of his casual interest in their content. Suddenly she felt very cold and pulled her cardigan tighter around her shoulders. What had been in those memos? She racked her brain. Nothing very significant, it seemed to her. Could there have been anything useful to a spy? The radio broadcasts were intended to be factual and informative, but she had heard that the Hungarian desk in Munich was overstepping its mandate, warning protesters not to back the moderate Communist Imry Nagy, and in one case actually giving instructions for homemade explosives. Her own office's communications with the State Department had made it very clear such commentators were out of line and that the radio broadcasts should in no way give the impression that America would intervene militarily to support the protesters.

She thought of this now, with the news about Vladimir. He'd known that! And he had somehow informed the Russians that if they invaded, there would be no matching action from Western powers. Her boring memos had had *everything* to do with the Soviet invasion. With shame, she thought of how Vladimir had looked at her. How she'd *thought* he had looked at her, when what he really wanted to see was the papers on her desk. Her cheeks burned.

The entire day, Helen longed for nothing more than a friendly ear to listen to her sort out her thoughts. When Mr. Major returned, he had nothing for her but a glaring eye and a stack of dictations. Pansy was not a listener. She spent the day asking questions about Vladimir out loud and then efficiently answering her own stupid questions. Helen thought, maliciously, that it was one of the few things at which Pansy was efficient. Besides gum chewing.

Helen went wearily home that night, looking forward to Rose's quiet companionship, but instead found a note saying she'd gone out for the evening and would see her in the morning. Helen thought of calling Thomas Lawson, but just as quickly, decided against it. He had been right, after all, thinking Vladimir was a spy. It was just too mortifying; she had the vaguest notion that after his surprise he might gloat. She wouldn't be able to stomach it.

***

She ended up visiting Clementine. It was a bit unusual to visit her seamstress, she knew, but she had sensed such a sympathetic spirit in her before. Clementine also had no connection to anyone but Helen, which felt discreet and comforting. So Thursday afternoon, after Mr. Major had left for Washington, and Helen's stack of dictation was down to a manageable size, she put on her hat and gloves and took the bus up to 81st Street. She had called Clementine that morning, but hadn't told her the reason for the visit.

"Is something wrong with the dress?" asked Clementine after they had greeted each other in her narrow hallway. She looked behind Helen as if she expected to see the dress trailing after her.

"No, no...it's perfect, it's wonderful. I wore it Saturday, you know......to the Emigré Ball. But I just...I wanted to...I don't know...I thought maybe..." Her voice trailed away and she stood there feeling awkward. She wished she hadn't come.

Clementine adjusted her glasses and gave her a long look through them. Then she stood to one side with a little smile and gestured down the hall.

"Come in, my dear. Why don't you sit down in the sitting room, and I will make us coffee, and then you can tell me what's bothering you."

As she sat waiting for the coffee, Helen felt her nerves already begin to relax. She felt a surge of happiness when Clementine arrived with the coffee and sat down to listen, but then fumbled and didn't know where to start. With embarrassment she began, apologizing that her visit had nothing to do with her dress or business or anything. She was suddenly aware of her imposition on Miss Cavaziel's time. But the latter was so encouraging in her manner, that soon Helen was telling her the whole story; not only about the sudden shock of Vladimir and her hopes dashed with it, but also of Heinrich. How lovely Munich with him had seemed at first and then how wrong things had gone. His expectations of a perfect, traditional German housewife, even though he'd brought home an American bride, the cruel things he had said to her when she failed, and her loneliness in a foreign country. Then came her job in the Munich office of The Committee, which Heinrich had intensely resented, and finally her decision to leave and transfer to New York. To start over.

"And then when I was finally getting settled here, finally getting to know someone who understood me, he turns out to be a spy! It's unbelievable! I even had to go in front of an interrogation squad yesterday and answer all their questions. They finally agreed that I wasn't his accomplice, but Oh, how unlucky I am! I am the unluckiest girl." She sat slouched in her chair, her hands folded, her tale told, born away dramatically on the wave of self-pity that it evoked.

Clementine didn't say anything.

After a moment, Helen concluded, "Anyway, I thought perhaps you would understand."

"Why me?" Clementine looked surprised for the first time since Helen had begun her story.

Helen sat up. "Well, you're a woman who's made a career. You're not married, and you've made a life for yourself on your own. And you came *here*, to New York City, independent, successful, and...and free. That's what I admire. It's what I want. But I seem to be making a mess of it."

"Ah, you thought...?"

"Well...I don't know." Clementine's quiet gaze was unnerving. Even more so than Vladimir's. Helen felt exposed, all her past, all her hopes, vomited out onto the coffee table between them. When she spoke again, her voice was very small.

"Don't you feel a little bit sorry for me?"

Clementine sighed and peered up at the painting on the wall a long moment.

"No, not much."

Her words hung in the air forever, and then she looked across at Helen and smiled.

"Yes, of course, a little bit. You are young, and life has given you big experiences to handle and asked a lot of you. But sorry for you? Life is a funny thing; we can't see all the turns it will make, and there are no guarantees. But we can't waste time feeling sorry for ourselves. There is already too much sorrow in life without us adding to it." She stopped and looked down at her hands, folded quietly in her lap.

Helen adjusted herself in her chair, but was silent. That was not the response she had expected. She didn't know what to say.

Suddenly Clementine clapped her hands together and looked up. "I suppose you wonder what I mean, and how I can dare say it. I mean an awful lot, I suppose." She put her head to one side thoughtfully, and pushed up her glasses to the bridge of her nose. "It's getting late. But when you have time, maybe Saturday, come back, and I'll tell you what I mean. I will tell you how I came to New York."

Chapter 11

The great church bell next door struck seven as Clementina unlatched the green wooden shutters of the bedroom she shared with her sister Catrina. Light swept into the small white-washed room, along with the smell of wood smoke from the morning fires in the village. As the tolling of the hours faded away, the higher sharp toll of the festival bell rang out, jubilant in the morning air. It was Ascension Sunday, the 12th of May, 1929, and Clementina waited there listening to the bell's reverberations rise in the clean air. From under the covers of the narrow double bed came a groan.

"Tina, close the window! It's too cold!"

"No, Catrina, it's time you were up, lazybones! And I think it will be our first really warm day. We need the encouragement after such a wet spring."

Two hours later they crossed the square from the big house to the church. The huge stone house at their backs had been purchased by her great-great-grandfather in the late 1700s when he'd returned from serving at the Vatican in the papal guard. How he'd amassed the wealth for such a purchase had been under discussion in the village through the intervening years, when each successive generation meant dividing the great house into smaller parcels. Clementina's family now had one small apartment and shared the house with three sets of cousins. In front of them, the elegant grey spire of the church shot heavenward in the blue spring sky, calling all parishioners from this part of the valley to worship.

The Cavaziels waited with the other village families on the square until the priest opened the great north doors and they all entered together in casual procession. For many families it was the last time in months they would worship together in church. Soon the men would take the cows up to the Maience and spend their summer in their tiny chalets, watching the herds and making cheese from the fresh milk. The Candinas children flocked around their mother while Signor Candinas talked with Signor Schmed. Gion Schmed, home from Chur for the holiday, visited with Pieder Decurtins and Anton Carigiet, his school friends, while their mothers chatted politely in a circle.

The late morning air was beginning to warm up. Spring came late here in the mountains, but when it finally arrived it came with the frenetic hum of nature coming alive, eager to grow and reproduce before the short alpine growing season was over. Today the air was full of this promise and of buzzing bees out searching for blossoms to pollinate.

In the church the deacon had opened the windows in the back of the sanctuary. During mass, the scent of the warming fields drifted in and mingled with the perfume of the incense that Pader Piedro used to bless them. It was nature coming to church to worship its Maker, thought

Clementina, just as it should. It was the kind of poetic thought that often passed through her mind, but that she would only sometimes share with Catrina. Their mother was too sensible for such things. Clementina now sat between her mother and sister in their usual pine pew on the eastern side of the church. Her two brothers sat next to Mumma, and little Barla nestled into Papa at the other end of the pew as mass began. It was sung in Latin, as usual, but that was close enough to Romantsch that Tina understood the sense behind the chanted words. Pader Piedro was a good priest who explained it all to the children at catechism, and who always greeted and blessed his congregation in their own language.

As the hour progressed, a ray of sunshine that had been shining in on the congregants at the front of the church crept slowly to the Cavaziels' pew. When it fell on her face, Clementina smiled and closed her eyes, basking in the heat and the rosy glow cast by the stained glass picture of Jesus and his first miracle at Cana. She breathed in the warm air, the mixture of the natural and the divine, feeling in that moment that her whole world was in harmony. The voice of the Pader lilted softly on.

"...for didn't our Lord say it? *Unless a grain of wheat falls to the ground and dies, it remains alone. But if it die, it bringeth forth much fruit.* Think of this, my people, in this planting season, that our lives, too, should be like the seeds that you sow, ready to plant and die each day for the good of those around us."

The homily ended. Clementina opened her eyes and the worshipers rose for the last hymn. As she stood, she saw Gion Schmed staring at her from the opposite side of the church, one row back. His eyes wide, his lips parted, he stood fixed as though he had seen a vision.

He waited for her outside the church door. When he asked if he could walk her home, she wasn't sure if he was teasing her, or if he'd forgotten who she was.

"Yes, I think so," she said, glancing at her father conversing with Signor Decurtins next to them. "But, you know," she said, nodding to their big house on the west side of the square," it will be a very short walk!"

"Ah yes, I...I know...," he fumbled awkwardly, looking down at his shiny leather shoes. They were city shoes. His ruddy cheeks blushed crimson and the color spread up to the roots of his curly dark hair. He started again, shyly. "I just thought...I just wanted..." Suddenly he raised his head and looked so intensely in Tina's eyes that she felt her stomach drop. For a second she saw what he wanted. Her. No one had ever looked at her like that before.

Then Gion flashed a broad, easy smile, his green eyes sparkling as he laughed at himself.

"Then we will have to take the long way!"

Chapter 12

It was the first of their Sunday walks, usually with Catrina along as well. Signora Cavaziel insisted that Catrina needed the exercise, but Clementina knew that Catrina was their unofficial chaperone. They would walk up the steep mountainside from the village to Nossadunna della Glisch, the beautiful red-steepled chapel built on the cliff to honor the Virgin Maria, then around by the Ferrera, which was fed by the glaciers on the Tödi, then tumbled down through Surrein and across to the other side of the valley where it joined the Rhine River.

In the middle of June, Gion came home for good, finished with his apprenticeship. He would help his father with the farm animals for the summer and then in the autumn begin work at the textile factory powered by the mill on the Ferrera.

Their walks became more frequent, and as the days grew longer he often called on her after supper. By then, Signora Cavaziel was willing to let them walk alone together, and Catrina was grateful to be released from her awkward chaperone duty. As they walked, they talked. They talked about everything, the people in the village, the books they read, the week's sermon, their favorite trees and flowers, their brothers and sisters, their plans for the future.

"I would have liked to be a farmer like my father," said Gion one evening in late June. "But my mother had plans for me, to work at the factory. She says if I can work well here for a few years, there may be an opportunity to move on to Chur perhaps, or even Zurich."

"But do you want to leave?" asked Clementina, surprised and turning quickly to look at him.

He sighed. "No, that is just it. I don't. This is my village, my mountain, my home. I don't have any reason to leave. Chur was far enough. And for what? I am happy here...when I am with the right person." He smiled down at her quickly, self-consciously, and then gazed up into the deep azure sky. Clementina smiled to herself, relieved. She felt the same way about Surrein.

"Catrina wants to go everywhere. I tell her she was born with itchy feet. She's always so curious about other valleys and other villages and is never satisfied until she's seen them for herself. She used to make us crazy begging to go to Ilanz. Then it was Chur. And now that she's been to Chur, she wants nothing more than to see Zurich someday."

"And you, Clementina? No itchy feet?"

"No... I like to read or hear about other places, but that's enough. I would be lost in a big city of people. I want to stay here in my home."

They stood still and looked together at the Alps rising up on either side of the valley, their sides impossibly steep.

The days were long now and the sun was still making its way toward the western end of the valley toward the Oberalp Pass. Here and there between the ridges that plunged to the valley floor, white peaks could be seen, snow-covered even in the height of summer. The mountainsides were covered with dark pine forests. Her father worked in those forests, long hard days cutting wood. Life was not easy here, but it was familiar, joyful, and good. She turned again to look up at Gion's broad honest face. Behind him rose the Tödi, huge, strong, reliable. Gion was right. With the right person, life here could be very good.

Chapter 13

The next Sunday, Gion was invited to dinner with the Cavaziel family. For the occasion, her mother had made capuns—her specialty—since the chard was well up in the garden. Clementina sat in the middle of one side of the table, with Gion judiciously on the other side, next to Catrina. Her parents, Giacan and Selena Cavaziel, sat closest to Gion, the better to engage him in conversation. At the other end sat Alfons with Dominik between him and Catrina. Barla was on Clementina's left and spent most of the meal trying to get her brothers' attention by kicking them under the table. The dinner conversation covered a range of subjects important to everyone in the village: the state of the crops after the late spring, the new cows Signor Schmed had brought up from Landquart, the plans for a new railway line over the pass. If Gion was at all uneasy, he didn't show it; he was polite, but seemed as comfortable conversing with her parents as she was.

"If they build the line to the Oberalp, they'll need workers, and heaven knows we could use the extra work in this valley," said Clementina's mother.

"If it ever happens," replied her husband. "Some of those railway chiefs are dreamers. The Oberalp isn't an easy pass to conquer."

"But they've even built a line up to the Jungfrau!" said Gion. "After that, our pass cannot be too terrible. If Hannibal made it over with his elephants, then I think the train builders will as well."

On the other end of the table, Dominik glanced at his parents, caught Clementina's eye, and started batting his eyelashes furiously at her. Alfons roared with laughter, and Barla cried, "What?! What's so funny!? I want to know what it is, too!" Clementina sighed. "It's nothing!" she hissed at her sister. "Be quiet!" she whispered to her brothers.

"But I didn't say a word!" protested Dominik innocently. Clementina looked to her other side, but the conversation carried on there just as before. This was the first time anything like courting had transpired in their household, and Alfons and Dominik were at the stage of adolescence where anything holding a hint of romance made them ridiculous.

After dinner there was a nut cake for dessert, with strawberries and cream. Clementina was pleased. She could tell her parents both approved of Gion, and he seemed so comfortable with her family that she had spoken little.

"Well, his manners are very good," said Signora Cavaziel when Gion had gone home and Clementina was helping her mother with the dishes.

"Ah, Mumma! There's more to life than good manners!" said Alfons, passing through the kitchen and grabbing a hunk of bread.

"Of course there's more than good manners. There's a good job, and Gion is sure to have one. How on earth can you be hungry again already, Alfons? You should think about what *you* will do when you have a family someday and need to feed all of them as well as yourself!"

Alfons tore off another piece of bread and danced out of the kitchen, just escaping Clementina's snapping dishcloth.

"Yes, Gion is sure to always have a good position, what with his training in the city," said Signor Cavaziel. He reached down to open the small door in the slate stove and blew on the embers. They glowed to life again, and when he touched them with a slim twig, a bright flame shot up like a flower. Giacan cupped the bowl of his white clay pipe protectively in his burly hand and brought the flame to it. He puffed to get the smoke going and then sat down heavily on the bench next to the stove. "But he's a good fellow. The big city hasn't made a mess of him. That's something." He puffed reflectively. "He still loves his home, doesn't he, little Clementina?" He looked up to where she stood leaning on the kitchen door frame next to him, wiping the last of the dishes, affection shining frankly in his warm brown eyes.

"Yes, Papa." She knew he would never say it aloud, but whenever she did marry and leave home, her father would wish for her to stay nearby.

"Yes, he's a good boy. A good man, I should say. Not that anyone could be good enough for my little Tina." He pulled on her long dark braid and chuckled into his mustache.

Then his head jerked up again and he fixed his dark eyes on her. "But all the same, guard your heart, little one. Wait for him to be clear with his plans."

"Yes, Papa." Clementina felt embarrassed at the warning. Her heart felt like a fluttering bird that flew off and landed where it wished. She could no more capture it and keep it than she could catch one of the wild Alpine sparrows and keep it in a cage in their chalet. Her heart. Where was it flying to now?

"Well, he is an intelligent young man, and sensible, too," said Signora Cavaziel from the doorway that led to the tiny kitchen. "You would always have enough to eat. What do his parents say?" asked Signora Cavaziel. She looked at Clementina and then glanced quickly at her husband.

"I think they are pleased," said Clementina slowly. "I think that they like me." She thought with pleasure of the day when Gion had walked with her to "meet" his father. Of course they already knew each other, but each understood that this meeting had more significance. Signor Schmed had been working in his second barn, the one in the pastures on the way to Campliun. He was wealthy enough to hire several hands, but he still maintained an active role in his own affairs, and had high work standards for his sons as well. But he was friendly and kind, and she'd left that meeting feeling well-liked and accepted. Signor Schmed had the same mossy green eyes as his son, and when he smiled, they crinkled up at the edges in just the same way. In the village, people said that he sometimes promised too much without following through, but they said it with good nature because it was also said that, with his kindness, he tried to make up for the coldness of his wife. It was true that Signora Schmed was a proud, austere person and that the younger village children did not like her at all. Clementina had never had a reason to fear her, but then, neither had she ever before had a reason to garner her attention. The Schmeds had one of the wealthiest farms and largest chalets in the village. Clementina was proud of her hardworking parents, but had to admit that they were not the kind of people with whom Signora Schmed liked to associate. Her parents planned and saved and there was always enough, but nothing more. Clementina did not pay much attention to what the villagers said—whether or not her mother was fashionable, whether or not her father's cows were old. After all, this was just as much her village, her valley, her mountains as anyone else's, rich or poor.

So she did not care much about Signora Schmed until one day, several weeks after Gion had started paying her attention. Outside the baker's shop, Clementina was just going in when the door burst open and out swept the black skirts of Signora Schmed. She stopped short.

"Clementina Cavaziel," she said simply and with finality. Her dark hair was pulled back into a bun so severe that the skin on her temples was taut. Her glittering eyes looked Clementina up and down.

"Bien di, Signora," said Clementina simply. She gazed calmly back into the older woman's dark eyes, but inside she quaked and wished she had taken more care with her braids this morning.

"Your parents are well?" Signora Schmed smiled, but only with the bottom half of her face. Her eyes shone coolly, just as before.

"Yes, thank you, very well."

"Hmmm." She paused and kept staring at Clementina as if she were a frock, sizing her up, taking her measurements. "Gion enjoys your company. But, you know, he will soon be very busy. His new work will not allow for distractions."

Clementina's face burned. *That's what she thinks I am! A distraction!*

"Of course." She mustered the courage to look earnestly and directly at Signora Schmed. "His work is very important. I..." She stopped. She didn't know what to say next.

"You will come to dinner soon," Signora said grudgingly. "We will talk then." With that, she swept off the shop step and regally down the street, the *a revair* she uttered with her back already turned ringing like a cheap trinket thrown from a rich woman's carriage.

Chapter 14

July flowed into the valley with light and warmth. Even before the village awakened and the tangy smoke from the village wood fires began to circle in the cool air, the sun had already bounded joyfully up above the mountain peaks into the clear pure sky. Wild strawberries were beginning to ripen in the thickets alongside the river, and in the meadows, angelica plants rose as high as Clementina's waist in their wild effort to go to seed before the days grew shorter again. Their large white flowers filled the hazy air with a scent like honey. The flat top of each one was covered with great numbers of bees in constant motion, like the crowd in the village square on Maria's Ascension Day before the procession to her chapel up the hill.

People said that their valley had short summers, but since Clementina knew no other kind, the brevity didn't bother her.

"I suppose our summers have to be short because they are so much more beautiful than anyone else's," she had once told Barla. "If they were longer, then the others would be upset and say it wasn't fair."

"What others, Tina?" asked little Barla.

"You know," she said, waving her hand vaguely. "The others, the ones who don't get to live here."

"The people who have to live down where it's flat?"

"Yes, dear, those poor people."

***

It was her favorite time of year. When she admitted it to herself, she felt slightly guilty, as if winter would find out and have its feelings hurt. She truly loved winter as well—sleigh rides up to Disentis, crossing the river when it froze over, the valley transformed to a mysterious world of white and black. The high, pointed, red steeple on Maria Glisch would look jaunty against the snow-laden fir trees beyond. But in the darker season, the mountains lost their kindly look and seemed fierce and distant. The days were short, hard, and cold and the long nights behind closed shutters were colder still. One didn't stray too far from home, and the wood fires in the big ceramic ovens in each chalet's sitting room never went out.

But ah, summer! That was what Clementina really loved. Then her mountains smiled down graciously again and invited visits to their lofty meadows and bright clear lakes. The gentian and edelweiss would be starting to bloom about now, thought Clementina as she started up the path leading to Maria Glisch and then beyond to the alp – the pastures high up on the mountain where the animals were taken to graze in the summer. Each village had its own community alp on the nearest mountain, and it was from this word that the whole mountain range—the Alps—had gotten its name. Clementina was going with Alfons today to take the goats up to pasture. The garden was weeded and the ironing was done and her mother had given her leave to go. She knew her eldest daughter loved to be outside and on the mountains in the summer. And besides, Selena Cavaziel surmised Gion was helping his brother with the cheesemaking on the alp today.

As Clementina and Alfons left the village and started to climb, they passed under the wild plum trees that grew along the steep dirt road. Hidden among the dark leaves were baby plums, hard and green. Last week Clementina had walked under this tree beside Gion. He had reached up and held one carefully, so it would not break off the branch.

"Mmm, plums! Plum cake is my favorite. You do know how to make plum cake, don't you? It's a requirement." He had turned to her as he asked, a quizzical look in his eyes, but a smile playing about his broad lips.

She didn't ask for what plum cakes were a requirement. Instead, she caught his gaze boldly.

"Of course I do. I promise I will make one just for you when the season is here." To herself she added that she would make it in their own kitchen, and in her imagination she saw the cake cooling on the table, greeting him when he came from the factory to their own home.

Gion had never talked about marriage openly, but in every subtle way the subject of a life together grew between them—places he would like to walk with her when the autumn leaves turned the lower mountainsides a thousand shades of color, sled rides they would take in the winter down the Schlans road, how he would show her the city of Chur, where he had lived and worked, the museum, the streetcars, and the shops where the fashionable ladies purchased their dresses. She, in turn, wanted to walk with him high up the alp on a clear day in the spring, when patches of snow still clung to the rocks, but the wildflowers were beginning their riotous dance of color in the fields. Each felt understood by the other; their mutual desire to walk together into the future was expressed in every possible way, except directly. But Clementina was willing to be patient. She knew the words would come, and she knew what her answer would be.

There could be no objection. The Schmeds owned a small chalet just behind their own that they had obviously kept for one of their children to live in. It would serve very well for them until they could save enough for something large enough for a growing family. Her own parents were very pleased with the idea of Gion as a son-in-law, and though the time she had spent at the Schmed home when she was invited for supper had felt stilted and uncomfortable, Clementina imagined that someday she, too, might initially be uneasy around the woman her son wished to marry. Gion's father was very kind, but also quiet, manifesting his authority as head of the household by silently nodding his agreement to whatever his wife and son said. Clementina decided that she would be confident and not mind Signora Schmed's distant ways. After all, her son loved her. She was absolutely sure of this; his unabashed, affectionate smile over the supper table–even in presence of his brother and sister—reassured her of this. Her eyes were wrapped up in his, drawing strength and confidence from his presence and attention. So she did not notice how Signora Schmed's sharp eyes also watched his gaze, nor did she hear Signora's quick intake of breath.

It is only a matter of time, Clementina thought as she walked behind Alfons and the goats. At the avalanche barrier above the village she stopped and leaned on her walking stick. Alfons was already a ways ahead up the path that ran alongside the ravine. He looked back, his dark curly hair ruffling in the breeze blowing down off the alp. She smiled and waved him on, and then stood, consciously slowing down her breath. It was a funny thing, but it seemed her lungs always made her stop and rest here, though she had hardly left the village. As she rose higher and fell into the rhythm of the climb, her lungs found their rhythm, too. Despite the thinner air as she rose in altitude up the steep mountainside, it was as if they functioned better at higher altitudes. It had always been like that, even as a child the spring after the terribly hard winter when she was eight, when she had contracted pneumonia. She had little memory of it, just vague recollections of her anxious mother placing her cool hand on Clementina's feverish forehead, the hideous acrid concoctions that burned against her skin, and the terribly itchy flannel they wrapped over her chest. She remembered, too, that the rest of the winter—while the other children played out in the snow—she had to stay close to the fire, her mother's soft brown eyes lighting in alarm anytime her hacking cough started again. The doctor had said that her lungs would never completely recover, but the following June she had insisted on walking in procession with the other children, to bring the village herds up to the alp. Her mother, following anxiously behind, had been astonished that with each step up, the climb seemed to grow easier for her little Clementina.

Her breathing slowed to a normal pace again and each breath was deeper. She stood atop the dike that formed a half moon across the rocky stream bed. There was a gap in the middle with a rough wooden bridge over it and the stream far below. The dike had been built by the villagers over the previous decade as avalanche protection. She turned and looked down at Surrein. It was already far enough below that it looked like the miniature town in a model railway village she had once seen in Ilanz. A piercing whistle rose through the air, and from down the valley to the east chugged the train, its red cars looking so trim and tidy and completing the impression of the miniature village.

The stream that ran under the little wooden bridge flowed from there over its rocky bed past the factory and on down through the heart of the village. Now, in midsummer, the water was very low. Another month and it would be just a trickle. But in late winter it was something else, and down this same ravine had swept many avalanches over the years, great walls of snow and rock, tumbling in an instant from high on the Tödi down to cover the village, destroying houses, farms and every living thing in its path. Thirty years ago the citizens of Surrein had started building the barrier after an avalanche had flattened 16 homes and barns and left 25 dead. The train line had been cut for weeks. The effort of building the barrier was worth it. It had succeeded in slowing the progress of subsequent avalanches, but it still wasn't enough. There was talk of building it bigger.

Clementina remembered the winter when she was 14, awakening early one morning to a sound like a giant train rumbling right past her pillow. When she opened the green shutters, in the dim light she saw that down in the field two barns had been swallowed up by the white mass. The peaks of their roofs poked up from the snow like grim islands, 100 meters from where they belonged. It had been spoken of as a small avalanche. One neighbor was killed.

It was the fury of the mountains and the hazard of living in their shadow. Clementina found it easy to understand why her pagan ancestors had revered and feared the mountains so much. When they rumbled and threw down their snow and ice, it was easy to imagine them as giant angry deities, taking out their wrath on the tiny humans who trembled at their feet.

Clementina held out her hands, palms up and at arms' length so that the distant village fit neatly into them. Everything and everyone she cared about was there. How she would love to know that she could always keep them safe. Then she remembered that one of the ones she cared about was higher up, so high above the ridge above her that he wouldn't even be able to see down to the village. With a smile, she turned quickly, her braid slapping against her cheek, and continued to climb.

Another 30 minutes brought her to the first of the mountain huts owned by the villagers. Five minutes after that the path led round a bend and past the Schmeds' chalet. She stepped off the path, her skirts swinging, and made her way over. Looking up the slope she saw Alfons, now a tiny figure in the distance, ascending quickly. He had known she would stop to see the Schmed brothers, and would not worry if she didn't appear soon.

"Hello!" she called out to the wooden hut and again as she drew near the door. "I brought you men something!" From her back she drew a small pack in which she carried some barley cakes she had made with her mother that morning.

She heard footsteps and then Gion appeared in the dark doorway. He looked surprised but happy to see her. Slowly, like the sun rising, he smiled. "There is only one man, and here he is."

"Where is Alois then? I thought you were helping him?"

"It turns out that he was helping me. And then father wanted him back down for something this afternoon."

"Oh," said Clementina, surprised, and now suddenly shy. Gion leaned on the door frame. His white shirt reflected the sun so brightly that it almost hurt her eyes.

They stood looking at each other in the bright light. The sunshine warmed the back of her shoulders, and there was the faint smell of clover. Aside from the quiet rustle of the wind in the grass, it was very still. She and Gion were alone together on this piece of mountain. In all this vastness—the hugeness of the mountains around them, the brightness of the sky above, so blue it tinged toward indigo—Clementine suddenly felt incredibly enormous, and then just as suddenly, utterly small. Her breathing had slowed when she stopped climbing. Now, looking into those eyes, green as the pine forest behind him, gazing steadily back at her, her breath came quicker again. So quiet and so still, yet the air between them resonated with energy. Then a bee, hurrying on its errand, buzzed between them as loudly as a train and broke the silence. Gion slowly stepped out of the doorway and down to the path, his eyes fixed on hers. Ever so gently, his hand touched her face as he bent to kiss her.

Chapter 15

They were bright golden days. Gion spent the long days on the alp while the herd grazed the mountain grasses, doing the milking and then following the careful steps that turned the fresh milk into hard cheeses that would keep during the winter. The Schmeds, whose large herd produced more cheese than they could consume, sent their big rounds of it to be sold as far away as Chur. Gion's workdays were long, but it was work that he loved, close to nature. As for Clementina, she always finished her work at home quickly, and then her feet rushed up the familiar path like mountain birds. The thrill of Gion's presence and touch made her waking and sleeping one long unbroken dream. Absolutely certain of their future together, she soothed the misgivings that began to germinate deep inside her about the intensity of those summer days. "*Do not awaken love before its proper time*," she had heard her mother admonish her and her sister over the past years, and until now she had never truly known what that meant. She loved Gion—heart, body, and soul—and was ready and willing to make his life her life. What was the proper time, if not now?

***

In late July, the days were growing shorter, and even with summer at its height, the long descent into winter began. An imperceptible sense of urgency crept into the air—urgency to complete the tasks of summer and daylight before the light was lost.

Despite the dark and the cold of the season, winter provided time for other things of beauty. In winter, there was finally time for long evenings by the woodstoves in each sitting room, time for mending, carving, singing, and just talking. The Cavaziel children loved to watch their father carve their pine furniture that he had built himself—hearts and flowers and leaves growing under his hands on the backs of chairs and around the frames of bookcases and wardrobes. Each piece had its own bouquet of decoration that made it unique, undeniably identifying the skill of its maker.

Snow would pile high on the houses until they would look like they were covered with a thick layer of whipped cream. The paths would get cleared as well as possible, but in the fields the snow was as high as Clementina's neck. The little red train would still shoot up the valley—with a snow plow attached to the front of the engine—but by late winter, if there had been no thaw, it chugged in between high white walls of built-up snow. The heat on the roofs of the houses melted enough snow to form enormous icicles that hung like monstrous fangs off the eaves.

After a heavy snowfall, when the weather cleared and the sun came out, the brilliance of so much light on so much snow was exhilarating. The air was sharp and one could hear the train whistle as far away as Tavanasa. On days like that, the cold air outside burned in the nostrils and in the lungs. In the afternoons after school, the children would drag their wooden sleds up the steep road that led to Schlans. Then they posted a sentry to watch for automobiles down where the Schlans road met the highway. The sentry would wave the all clear with a red scarf, and then the sledders leapt on their sleds and hurtled down like lightning bolts. Motor cars were a rarity in the mountains, and even more so in the winter. Nevertheless, the odd adventurous driver sometimes took on the mountain roads and would be thinking more of the treacherous conditions than the possibility of village children on sleds crossing their path. For the children, the possibility of collision with an automobile at the end of the perilous descent made the experience that much more thrilling.

In winter, Giacan Cavaziel worked short intense days in the few hours of daylight. He and the other woodcutters trudged through the forest on snowshoes, carrying long heavy saws. They worked in teams, felling snow-laden pine and firs and piling them where horse teams would later drag them back to the mill on the river. As dark fell, Giacan returned home, soaked through all his layers of wool stockings and wrappings and chilled through his skin. Selena Cavaziel made him sit on the bench next to the stove, and she unwrapped the woolen strips from his stiff legs while tiny icicles hanging from his mustache would melt and drip from the heat. Though she never spoke of it, her face showed relief each night when he reappeared at the door. It was difficult and dangerous work. She knew that he was a careful man who wouldn't take unnecessary risks, but even so, there was always the danger of an avalanche. Avalanches buried the cautious and the careless alike.

But for now, the long nights of winter still lay far away. Their cold shadows had not yet stretched to touch the two figures making their way down the path in the fading light, the two young lovers for whom time seemed to stop each moment they were together and to last an eternity each moment they were apart. Gion and Clementina had stayed on the mountain longer than usual today, losing their sense of time and responsibility in their intoxication with each other. Below them, purple twilight washed the valley in softness, and by the time they finally strolled, hand in hand, into the streets of the village, only the tips of the peaks at the far west end caught the last fiery bits of sunlight. Gion walked Clementina to the door of her house and stopped. Behind the curtains of the Cavaziel sitting room there flashed a quick movement, but neither of them noticed. It would be completely improper for Gion to kiss her goodnight here in such a public place. But gazing up at him she thought of how soft his lips had felt against hers that afternoon, the strong feel of his arms wrapped around her, and the touch of his brown hands on her skin.

"Goodnight, darling Clementina," he spoke softly. "Will you come to see me again tomorrow?" Looking down at her, his eyes shone bright with a mixture of hunger and fulfillment. "You can help me with the cheese, now that Alois is working the hay down here with father."

The look he gave her made her head spin, like the thick wine she was allowed to drink at holidays. What wouldn't she do if only he would always look at her like that? She wanted him, to be wholly his, to make him wholly hers. Her feelings were so great in that moment, looking at him in the beautiful summer twilight, she couldn't trust herself to speak. He reached out and ran the back of his index finger down the side of her cheek.

She felt tears forming in her eyes, whether tears of joy and happiness or of frustration with her own feelings and her own weakness, she wasn't sure. He waited still, his dark head to one side, his green eyes imploring. Her stomach felt like one of Alfons' goats had kicked her. Shutting her eyes, she nodded quickly and ran into the house.

Inside the door her mother was waiting.

"Clementina," she said in exasperation, "you are very late home!" She paused. "I saw you and Gion out the kitchen window. The two of you shouldn't behave like that in public when he has not yet spoken to your father!"

Squeezing back her tears, Clementina looked at her mother and saw more worry than anger on her face. Her mother had surely seen how Gion had gazed at her, consuming her with his eyes. Perhaps she guessed.

"Mama...I..."

Her mother stepped over and wrapped Clementina in her arms. She stroked her daughter's long, dark, thick braid and whispered into her ear, "Child, I know you care about him deeply, but please walk very carefully. He has promised you nothing. Guard your heart, daughter. *Do not awaken love before its proper time.*"

Chapter 16

The week that followed was a beautiful one, as was the one that followed that. Day after day was a happy dream for Clementina. Each day she did her work quickly and in anticipation. With a goal at the end of it, the washing and the ironing were done easily and cheerfully, and when she baked she always made something extra to carry up to Gion at the end of the afternoon. Sundays after Mass and the midday meal, they met for long rambling walks along the Rhine, taking Clementina's siblings along. And at the wide place where the green glacial water ran calmly over the shallows, they sat on boulders at the river's edge and dipped their feet in the frigid water, so cold it made their ears ache. The river widened here in their part of the valley, but Gion could still throw a stone and hit the trees on the other side.

"Teacher told us the Rhine is one of the most important rivers in Europe!" said Barla proudly.

"He said that here it is just the Baby Rhine, but when it grows up up north even big ships and barges go on it."

"It is not a *baby*," retorted Dominik indignantly, "it's a great river here, just the way it is!"

"Well, Teacher has been to Basel, and he said that there the Rhine is so wide you can barely see someone standing on the other side. And he said that that is not even the widest part. And he's the Teacher, and he knows. So there."

Dominik said nothing more, but turned away moodily. The teacher was the teacher and must know what he was talking about, but Dominik still felt protective of their river, his river, that in his view was just about as perfect a play place as a boy could want. He turned back to the construction of the dam that he and Alfons had begun. Gion suddenly jumped down and into the water, getting his trousers soaked, and splashed over to help the boys with their project. Clementina and Catrina sat and watched, swirling their bare feet in the cold water. It was funny, thought Clementina, in a valley that was so peaceful and calm, here was this river that was always on the move. Even in the dead of winter when it froze half over, underneath the ice, the water still kept flowing, going to see far off places they had all only heard about.

"I should put you in the water in a basket, like Moses," she said to her sister. "Then you could travel off to everywhere you want to go."

"It's a nice thought, isn't it?" answered Catrina. "I was just thinking the same thing. That if only people would throw all their troubles in the water, and then the river could carry them far, far away. This water goes from here, all through Switzerland, to Lake Constance, through Germany, to the

North Sea and then out into the ocean and the whole world. Amazing! I wonder what it's like, the ocean," she added dreamily.

Clementina smiled at her. "Don't worry, Catrina, someday you'll see it. Probably sooner than you think."

Chapter 17

Clementina opened the shutters just as the church bell rang out the hour. Light flooded the room, and with it, a change in the air. The morning air was no longer as cool as it had been in July; the mountains were holding onto the sun's heat, and the nights were not as refreshing now that it was August. Up the valley toward the Oberalp, Clementina saw the haze typical of these later summer days already forming.

"Wake up, slugabed!" she called to Catrina. The form under the feathers groaned and moved.

"Oh, Clementina! It's still early; even Papa is sleeping late these days!"

"Early! Gracious! I've been up an hour already and my chores are halfway done!"

"Hmmm..." complained the form in the bed. "You're only so busy so you can go up to see Gion earlier." Catrina flopped the bedcover down and her dark eyes twinkled at her sister. "At least one of us has a beau," she sighed dramatically. Clementina smiled and blushed. Despite the long lovely weeks since their first walk after Mass, she still felt shy talking about the fact that Gion had chosen her.

"Has he spoken to Papa yet?" asked Catrina suddenly, her head tilted to one side. "He ought to."

"No, he hasn't," answered Clementina. Catrina was only voicing what her whole family wondered, but as time wore on, their constant questioning glances annoyed her. She was tired of always having to speak for him, when she knew he would soon speak for himself. Why wouldn't they trust him like she did? She was sure of his intentions, and her family needed to be patient like she was. Indeed, he had been so agitated when she saw him on Saturday that she had begun to hope he would ask to speak to her father Sunday afternoon. How surprised she had been when he'd found her after Mass to tell her quickly that he couldn't walk with her that afternoon as his mother had made plans. They had unexpected guests. Would he see her tomorrow? Disappointed but untroubled, she promised that he would, and he rushed away. It was the least they had spoken to each other in a day in weeks, and she hurried through the rest of Monday's work with eagerness until the moment when she could start her climb up the mountainside.

Despite her anticipation, she walked slower than usual today. The air was heavy, and the sun beat hotly through the haze onto her shoulders. The sultry air of these days was harder on her lungs, and her breaths came shallower and shallower. She stopped alongside the Ferrera to rest and scoop a drink of water from the clear stream. Even the birds were quiet today. Only the insects buzzing and the stream's gurgle made any noise. Another quarter hour and she stepped off the main track onto the path to the Schmeds' chalet.

One of their cows stood in the path. Clementina slapped her tawny backside to get her out of the way. The cow moved slowly and then turned around to look at her reproachfully with its huge limpid eyes. Rounding the last bend, she saw the small wooden hut on the knoll ahead of her, facing out and down over the valley far below. Her heart leapt at the familiar sight and the thought of her Gion in whose arms she would fall in a few moments. He had gotten used to looking out for her at this time of day, as he finished the work on the morning's milk. She looked eagerly for his arm raised in greeting.

Instead, as she watched, another figure came out of the hut. Shorter and fairer, it was Alois who stepped out and then back inside without glancing in her direction. She moved back in the shade of some pine trees and listened for him to speak to his brother. The silence of the heat covered the mountainside, and hardly a breath of wind even stirred the branches above her. She heard nothing. Wondering what to do, she continued more slowly. Alois was friendly enough, but she still felt awkward interrupting the brothers at their work. As she hesitated, Alois walked out and took up the walking stick leaning against the door. He stepped off lightly on the path and headed in the opposite direction, up beyond the hut where most of the cows were grazing. Clementina saw that no other herding stick was there. She waited until Alois' figure was tiny and disappearing behind the rocks a ways up the hillside. Then, quickly, she walked to the hut and peered in the open window. The cheesemaking tools were set out neatly on the table where Alois had placed them, and the molds were on the shelves behind, but no one else was there.

Back down in Surrein, Clementina turned off the path at the top of the village and walked toward the Schmeds' large chalet. On the walk back down, her annoyance had turned to concern. Gion was certainly ill and therefore hadn't gone to the alp today. It was true he hadn't seemed himself yesterday, almost feverish. Such an illness in summer was worrisome.

Sure enough, as she approached the large house she could see the shutters on the top floor where Gion slept with his brother were closed. Her heart beat faster. Of course she had no claim on him that would require telling her of his illness, but still, it would have been kind. She would like to think she had the right to help care for him.

She raised the heavy iron knocker and hesitated, not wishing to awaken her dear Gion if he were sleeping. She didn't need to. Instantly, she saw the face of Gion's sister, Esther, at the parlor window near the door. Clementina lowered the knocker carefully. She smiled at Esther and waited for her to open the door. Instead, the window scraped open and she stuck out her head. She smiled a polite smile at Clementina.

"Ciao, Clementina."

"Ciao, Esther. Is he alright? Is he sick?" she asked a little hurriedly. "Gion, I mean." She blushed stupidly at the sight of Esther's placid face. "I thought I would see him today. He said he would see me."

"He is quite well. I'm sorry, though, he cannot see you right now." Esther studied the red geraniums in the window box in front of her. "It's so very hot today, isn't it? Do you think it will continue? I should really water these flowers. Bien di, Clementina."

Esther's head disappeared inside the house, and Clementina stood on the steps in front of the closed door feeling like a tiny child, dismissed after punishment. It was so strange. Confused, she turned and walked slowly home.

Chapter 18

The next day she waited for Gion to come or for some message from him. It seemed such a petty thing; only two days had gone by since Sunday, it wasn't really that long. She chided herself for feeling his absence so keenly, but for the past two months, hardly a day had gone by when she hadn't seen his handsome smiling face for at least a few minutes.

Wednesday afternoon she could bear it no longer, and she steeled herself and returned to the Schmeds' doorstep. This time Signora Schmed answered. The look on her face was enigmatic. Clementina only hoped that her own face could cover her emotion so well. For the first time, as she looked into Signora Schmed's eyes, she allowed herself to admit the thought that she had so often pushed away: this woman was not kind.

"Yes?" asked Signora Schmed, as if she had no idea why Clementina would be calling.

"Bien di, Signora, I came to ask after Gion. I have not seen him for a few days. I thought he must be ill."

"I am sorry, dear child. He is not here. He is very well, and has gone to visit his uncle and aunt in Chur. It was an honor for them to invite him, and so he must pay our respects to our relatives in the city."

"Oh," answered Clementina hesitantly. She forced herself not to show surprise. "Yes, of course. He will be back in a few days then?"

"I cannot say when he will return. I will go myself this weekend to join them. I will tell him you inquired after his health. It was very kind of you to ask. Good day, Clementina. Please greet your parents for me."

"Yes, of course. Good day, Signora Schmed."

Clementina walked back through the village, stunned. Gion had never mentioned such a trip to her. It had not been planned, she was sure of it, or he would have said something. He would have told her. Suddenly, all her efforts to please Signora Schmed—to appear fine enough and to be accepted—seemed completely futile. Clementina was disliked, not for anything she had done, but for who she was. Her family had nothing but character, good reputation, and hard work. She had tried hard to please the woman who was to be her mother-in-law—for the sake of her son—to dress the right way, to act the correct way, to say the right things. In response, she had now been spoken to with the cold distance of a stranger.

She went home quickly, thinking she would write Gion, then realized that she had no address at which to write him. And what could she say, anyway? She would have to wait.

A letter arrived the following day.

My dear Clementina,

I am writing as quickly as I can and will write more very soon. My uncle has called me here on urgent business. He distrusts his bookkeeper and wants me to ensure the work is correct. It is very dull work, and I think it will only take a few days, but my mother will come on Saturday and wants me to show her the city. I am miserable to be here and away from you. We will come home as quickly as I can manage it.

Your Gion

It was one of the few things she had that was written in his solid handwriting. She folded it back up and kept it in her dress pocket the rest of the day. Here was tangible proof of his affection for her. "I am miserable to be away from you," he had said. She was a whirl of miserable because he was miserable, but it was combined with delight that he was miserable on her behalf.

So she waited and worked. Gion's letter comforted her—she reread it often—but waiting for word from him was still agonizing. The August heat was oppressive, but the Cavaziel house had never been cleaner or the laundry so well cared for. No one in her family dared ask; they waited too.

"Go with Catrina and the others to the river," said her mother the following Thursday afternoon. The heat was so great that they had let the fire in the stove burn out. They would eat cold sausage and dried beef for supper. "Cool your feet in the water. It will do you good."

"No, Mama, I would rather stay here. There is still the ironing to do."

Her mother came around the table and put her hands on Clementina's shoulder, looking her in the eyes.

"Child," she said in a tone Clementina remembered from the time she was a small girl, "the ironing can wait. We will do it in the morning when it is cooler. Go."

So she went. They spent the hottest hours of the day by the cold, green water, Catrina and Clementina with their feet in a shallow pool and their backs against a huge boulder that had broken down off the mountain in some past catastrophe and rolled onto the sand bar at the edge of the river. Barla, Alfons, Dominik, and other children from the village were at work again on the dam, trying to make a calm pool in which to swim. Clementina couldn't help thinking about the last time she'd been here with Gion, the way he played with her brothers and teased Barla, how well he fit into their family. She willed herself to stay in the moment, to feel nothing but the sun on her shoulders and her toes in the water. Catrina asked her nothing about Gion, and she was grateful. For a short while, she made no plans for the future, nor any reflections on the past; for a few moments she just *was*.

Walking home, Clementina did feel better. Her mother had been right. The air was beginning to cool off, her breathing was easier. It would all come right in the end, she was sure. She fell behind the others walking home, enjoying the golden light and the odor of drying hay wafting from the fields. There was a man leading a horse down the main road, which met the river path at the fountain. He had his hat down low, to shield his eyes from the low western light, but as they drew closer to one another and he lifted his head, she saw it was Gion's father, Signor Schmed. She felt her heart jump, but she was genuinely happy to see him. He was always kind, and his face looked so much like his son's. But if he saw her, he didn't show it until they were nearly abreast. He looked out across the field of pasture, then down at the road.

"Signor Schmed!" Clementina called out. "Buona sera!"

"Ah, Clementina," he said, nodding his head and stealing a glance at her eager face. "Ah, Clementina," he said again slowly. Then he stopped and stood and looked down the road. "I...I am sorry, Clementina. You are such a sweet girl." He looked at her quickly once again, a small smile on his lips, but his eyes were sad. Then he turned and started walking on his way again.

Clementina stood speechless and watched him go. The early evening heat was still stifling, but something inside suddenly felt very cold.

Chapter 19

August gave way to September, and though the days grew perceptibly shorter, the heat wave engulfing the Alps carried on. At Mass on the first of September, Father Piedro added prayers for rain to quench the thirst of the farmers' crops and the village's gardens. It was no rote exercise; the stream through the village was drying up. Except for the glaciers, the snow had melted off the mountains above and all that showed was great dry rock. No water for the garden meant less food in the larder for the winter. No rain for the pasture meant less milk from the cows and less cheese and meat. To Clementina, sitting on the bench with her family, the incense-filled air was heavy and oppressive. Every window in the church was open, but not a breath of air moved and the smoke rose only slightly from the censer before trailing slowly about the old priest's robes. The odor pinched Clementine's nostrils and made her restless.

There were fewer worshipers today than usual, as many families who could afford it had gone down to the lakes to escape the heat and to visit relatives. A few rows ahead, the pews where the Decurtins family and the Cavigelli family usually sat were empty. The Cathomases, who sat on the other side of the aisle and just behind them, were also gone. In the row behind that, Signor Schmed sat alone. The Mass slowly inched along, the priest singing the familiar words of forgiveness in Latin. Their own language was so close to Latin that she could always understand the meaning, but today Clementina couldn't keep her mind in church. Sitting still was an enormous effort. She longed to wave her hand to clear the air of the oppressively sweet odor of incense. How could the time move so slowly?

Monday morning, Gion had been gone two weeks. There would be mail delivery today, and surely some message from him, Clementina thought, as she went out to do the marketing for her mother. Basket in hand, she opened the door at the baker's shop. Their own bread was gone, and with the heat, her mother had not baked on Saturday. The bell on the door tinkled and the village women stopped their clucking for a moment to turn and say "Bien di" in her direction. Then they turned and resumed their gossip, like so many hens in the barnyard. Clementina waited patiently, lost in her own thoughts, until she heard the baker's wife raise her voice to speak to the woman at the head of the line. She wrapped the woman's bread slowly in brown paper, speaking loud enough for everyone in the shop to hear.

"Have you heard the news? There will soon be a wedding! Gion Schmed is engaged to marry Flurina Decurtins, the mistral's daughter! And quickly, too; they have ordered a cake for Saturday after next. What a match that will be! Apparently he chased her all the way to Chur."

Amid the chorus of astonished 'ohs' from the women in the bakery, the baker's wife slid her narrow eyes quickly to Clementina. Clementina felt her heart thud and almost stop. What nonsense! What was this woman talking about?! Everyone in the village had seen her together with Gion. She grew hot with indignation at such a ridiculous mistake.

"It will be an enormous cake," continued the baker's wife. "And in this heat, too! How shall I keep it from melting? I certainly hope the weather breaks before then!"

No! Clementina bit the inside of her lip to keep from crying out. It couldn't be true. What could it mean? Her breath came in short gasps that sounded deafening to her. She had to leave the shop, to run. She felt the eyes of the baker's wife on her again. Clementina looked up. The woman's mouth was turned up on one side with the merest hint of a smile, as if she enjoyed watching the confusion her news inflicted. She couldn't leave, not with this meddling woman waiting for exactly that response. Clementina's anger supplanted her shock. She forced her breathing to be calm and waited her turn, focusing her attention on the brown skirt of Signora Candinas at the counter in front of her. Finally, it was her turn. Her voice was not as steady as she wished it to be as she asked for a brown paun loaf, nor when she said her *Engraziel* in thanks before leaving. But she looked the baker's wife in the eyes, daring her to find anything troubled in her own. They were wrong. They were wrong! There was some reasonable explanation. Gion would send a message explaining the mistake.

As she walked through the village, her heart beat faster and faster as her anger rose in defense of Gion. The sun was already high and hot and the air humid and still. Perspiration trickled from under her braids and down her neck. In the square in front of the church she passed old Signora Vincenz with hardly a nod and pulled herself up the already hot stone steps to the main door of her family's house. Inside, the cool dark hall felt like a relief. She opened the next door into the Cavaziel sitting room and flung the bread on the table. Leaning back on the door to close it, Clementina closed her eyes and let out a long breath. Footsteps came quickly from the next room. Not her mother, but Catrina. Her sister burst in from the kitchen.

"Have you heard what they are saying in the village, Tina?" Catrina cried. "It can't be true! I don't know why they are saying such lies! Gion loves *you*!"

Clementina opened her eyes and the heaviness Catrina saw in them was her answer. Catrina stood waiting for Clementina to say something, to respond. She parted her dry lips.

"I..." she started. Then she stopped and fell into her sister's arms.

Chapter 20

By midday Tuesday, the heat still hadn't broken. A thick haze filled the air from the Oberalp down to Ilanz and the details of the ridges beyond the lowest ones were blurred. Thunder rumbled in the tops of the mountains, but the air was as heavy and still as ever. The air in the small rooms that made up the Cavaziel part of the house was stuffy, and though Clementina and Catrina opened all the windows and wedged them tight against the sill, not a breath of wind whispered through their rooms.

At midday, Signor Cavaziel came with Alfons from the field where they'd been scything hay for Signor Cathomas. He sat wearily at the table and took a long drink from the glass of water that was set for him. Clementina took the cornmeal polenta her mother had prepared and put it on the table. The family sat quietly around it, the heaviness of the air outweighed only by the heaviness inside them. Signor Cavaziel said grace and, in unison, they made the sign of the cross.

"It is true," he said finally, staring down at his plate. "Gion Schmed is engaged to Flurina Decurtins. I have heard it from her uncle, the station master. Her father went to Chur this morning to conclude the arrangements. The wedding will be on the fourteenth."

Signora Cavaziel stopped in the middle of serving her family, her spoon hung in midair.

"Giacan?" Her voice was high and unnatural as she spoke her husband's name.

He sighed long and bitterly, raising his arms and letting them fall.

"I do not know what to think, Selena."

He lifted his eyes and looked into Clementina's. She stared across at him, but as if she saw nothing. Her dark eyes were clouded and faraway. Finally she focused on him.

"May I be excused, Papa?" Clementina asked slowly, her voice hardly more than a whisper. Her father nodded gently, and Clementina rose, walked to the door, and went outside. From the other side of the door behind her she could hear the stunned silence break as her brothers and Catrina asked all the questions they had been holding back the past two days.

Out the door and down the stone steps she ran, across the main road, out of the village and up the path to Mariaglisch. Under the plum tree she passed, its boughs now heavy with purple fruit. Some had fallen onto the path, where no one had ventured to gather them in this heat. In her haste Clementina trod on them, slipping in their ripe juices up the steep incline. On she went, around the bend to the barrier.

Her breathing became heavy and ragged, but she continued up.

The air was cooling rapidly and above her a distant rumbling sounded high on the Tödi, but she took no notice. For over an hour she climbed, willing herself to think nothing, to notice nothing but each blade of grass along the way. On she went, her breathing now regular to support the steady rhythm of her climbing legs. Past the Maiensäss, past the chalets, up through the forest to the last line of trees. The path faded away into grass and rocky ledge. Clementina walked over to the edge of the ridge and looked down into the gorge, thousands of feet below. The wind was picking up now, and higher still the dark gray thunderclouds rolled over the saddle from the northern side of the Alps. Down they poured into that chasm of gray, heartless rock. Falling, falling down slopes now cold from the wind, all the heat of the previous days suddenly swept away. She stood on the precipice, nothing and no one visible now from the village so far below. She stood, as still and gray as granite herself and saw the thunderclouds moving over and swallowing her up in their surge to the bottom of the valley.

The air felt like a live thing on her skin, and there was a faint smell of burning. The electricity in the air around her crackled and the roots of her hair stood on end. Startled, she stepped back from the edge of the crevasse and peered into the dark cloud. It roiled in on itself, but moved steadily onward, as if in all that darkness and mystery rode a mighty presence. Clementina sank to the grass. Suddenly, just below her, a brilliant flash lit up the treetops and immediately exploded, like the sound of a thousand trains running next to her. Clementina flung her face to the ground and covered her head with her arms to shut out the noise. *They will worry about me out in this*, she suddenly thought of her family. A huge drop hit the back of her neck, then another and another, and now with the flood of rain fell her tears, as ceaseless as the storm. Into the unmoving mountainside her shoulders shook, and the parched grass soaked up her pain.

Chapter 21

The downpour lasted three days. When the clouds finally exhausted themselves, Clementina found that she, too, was empty. Empty of tears and empty of feelings. All that was left inside her was a dull ache and the vast emptiness. The weather turned and the days were beautiful. They were again sunny and warm, but in the air was a touch of crispness that hinted at fall. Despite all that she had felt and the emotions she had subsequently killed over the last three days, in a small detached part of Clementina's heart she couldn't help but be happy with the weather for Flurina's sake. Maybe it would be easier, she thought, to be angry at Flurina, but she couldn't bring herself to be. Flurina was a sweet, simple girl and she was as caught in the schemes of her own mother and Gion's as Clementina was herself. Instead, Clementina felt that in a surreal, vicarious way Flurina was going to live the life with Gion that Clementina should have had. But as the first week of September came and went, Clementina began to suspect it would be she who would bear his first child.

A letter came from Gion. It rambled on about duty and family. *He was sorry*, he wrote, *if he had given her the wrong impression about his intentions.* It was written, Clementina knew, with his mother standing over his shoulder. She was an ambitious and conniving woman, but she understood the importance of appearing civil. Clementina read the letter once and then threw it bitterly into the fire. It was not from the Gion she knew. The Gion she had known.

He came to the house after he and his mother and Flurina's family returned to Surrein. His mother was out and he had briefly escaped her oversight to knock at the Cavaziel's door. Catrina had seen him coming across the street and warned Clementina, who hid in the bedroom, crouched on the floor, clutching her pillow to her chest. He wanted to explain, to say goodbye, he told a tight-lipped Catrina, as if he could somehow make right what he had already done. Catrina had sent him away through a half-closed door.

"She's not here. She's gone to Ilanz."

The next day, it was her father who met Gion at the door.

"She does not want to talk to you, Gion. You have already made your intentions clear."

Listening from the other side of the house, Clementina felt her heart beat faster. She could only hear her father's voice, but she knew Gion stood there, waiting to talk with her. Suddenly she jumped up, about to run down the hall to the door and into his arms. To see his sweet face, his eyes looking at her with love and desire. He would be hurt, hearing that she didn't want to speak to him, and she longed to comfort him. She heard her father close the front door with a bang, and she stood still, her hand on the door handle, fighting down her desire. There was no use. There was nothing she could change now.

Chapter 22

The fourteenth dawned bright and clear. As was the village custom, the wedding was published as a public church service and anyone in the village could attend. The church was full to bursting. On the train from Chur came Gion's aunt and uncle who had helped bring about the happy event. The bride was calm but smiling radiantly. If she had discovered that her groom's heart had belonged to another until recently, no one would ever suspect it by looking at her. She had family and fortune; she was the *mistral's* daughter. But she was meek and quiet and would, no doubt, always do whatever her mother-in-law required.

From her girlhood, Flurina had admired Gion from a distance. Her mother had always intimated that he was the only boy in the village worthy of her family's position. When their mothers schemed to put the two young people together in Chur where Flurina vacationed with her parents, the young woman took events as a matter of course. It never occurred to her to distinguish between the affections of her supposed suitor and those of his fawning mother. When Signora

Schmed had implied to her that her son's polite attentions meant a proposal of marriage, with her mother's encouragement she was happy to accept. Gion found himself caught between a misinterpretation to Flurina on one hand and his forceful mother—full to the brim with tearful sermons on duty and debt to family—on the other. Try as he might, he could not make his mother listen, and she had no intention of losing control over him. In the end, he wished only to make her weeping cease and to make his mother happy. On his wedding day, he stood handsome and tall and smiling, but his heart was enveloped in the numbness that had swallowed it two weeks before.

Clementina could not stay in the village. Across the street and up the path she trudged. Once again, up the hill to Mariaglisch she went. Across the path hung the familiar branches of the wild plum tree. The fruit had all fallen off, and what hadn't been gathered lay in rotten clumps on the ground, wasps buzzing hungrily in the sickly sweetness. Just above the chapel was a bench where she and Gion had sat and talked once on a Sunday afternoon. She sat down there now. The village lay before her, small and distant, yet close enough to make out each distinct house, each well-known alleyway, the people hurrying into the church. She pulled her legs up onto the bench and hugged her knees. Down below, she could make out a figure in white, waiting in front of the door on the arm of a tall man in a suit. She turned away and started climbing again.

She only stopped when she reached the ridge where the rainstorm had caught her two weeks ago. The mountains around her were sunny and benign now, their peaks raised in the sunny blue skies like the faces of happy schoolchildren. Clementina loved these mountains. They were her mountains. But today it felt like they were mocking her. For the first time in her life, as she looked around at them, she felt like they were closing her in. They had always cared for her. Certainly they were dangerous and unpredictable, but they loved her, she knew. She had always felt safe here. Until now. These mountains, this valley, that village, those people. She felt them wrap around her like a bandage around her chest and begin to squeeze.

Her chest tightened and her breathing came in fits. She sank to the ground, sitting on the hard rock. The cows were at the Maiensäss farther down the mountain now that the days were shorter, and the sound of their bells didn't reach up this far. The only sound was the swooshing of the breeze and an occasional bird cry. In the meadow around and below her, the bluebells and poppies that grew wild were near the end of their cycle, dropping seed pods that would wait under the blanket of snow until awakened by next spring's sunshine.

There was a life waiting inside her, too, she was sure of it now. *And what kind of life will this child have?* she thought bitterly. The truth of her situation hit her swiftly and fully, cutting through the fog of disappointment and sadness that had surrounded her since the day Gion had left so suddenly.

She would have a fatherless child in a small village where everyone knew everyone else's secrets. She loved the people in the village like extended family, but she couldn't bear the thought of them all pointing and talking, whispering at every street corner. And her child? What life could he have? He would be a bastard, shunned at worst and forever pitied at best, given no advantages in life, always working hard but never reaping recognition. He would be fatherless, because honestly, who would ever love her again? She would be shunned herself. Even if everyone knew who the baby's father was, she would be the one held responsible, not Gion.

It occurred to her that she had grounds to have Gion's marriage annulled, if he would admit that he was the baby's father. Everyone else would know he was. But to do that, she would have to speak out publicly and ask her father to speak out for her. She thought of her parents' pain, how much they endured in life already. She knew that her father certainly would speak up for her, though it would cost him the little honor he had in the village.

And Gion? Would he still love her after she dragged him through that? She loved him, but after everything, she felt deep pity and anger that he had conceded to his mother in the end, giving up the woman he supposedly loved. Even if she could have him back, she wondered if she could ever respect a husband that she pitied. And his family? A mother-in-law who disliked you might eventually be won over, but one who despised you for the shame you brought her family would despise you forever. And Flurina. Clementina had no particular love for her, but in the end, what had she done to deserve that kind of public shame? She would have shame enough anyway when her husband's baby was born to another woman.

She cursed herself for her naiveté, for her gullibility and her foolishness. How could she have been so self-serving not to think clearly? How could she have not seen how her thoughtless moments would eventually affect everyone around her? It seemed so obvious now. She had not thought clearly then, those lovely ridiculous days in Gion's arms, but she would now. She had lost her self-control then, but never again.

Clementina put her face in her hands and tried to think clearly what would be best for everyone. She thought again of her family, of the bride Flurina, of her own future and of her baby. The whirl of thoughts and situations tumbled one over another in her mind, every path she might choose seemed blocked, hemmed up with stones like the granite around her. Her hands against her face smelled like earth, like the mountain. She cried out a sob of despair into the wind. The breeze moved around her, carrying her cry out and down into the valley. Just as quickly, it swirled on itself and back up it came, bringing with it another sound, the sound of church bells. The wedding service had finished. Gion and Flurina Schmed were husband and wife.

With each stroke, finality and loss struck her heart. But something else as well. The sound thudded determination into her breast. She would not stay in this village with them; she would not give that future to her child. She would leave. She stood and looked wildly around her, at the green slopes, at the plunging valley, at the glistening peaks of the Alps, at the Tödi behind her, her mountain. She would let them all go. She would leave them.

Chapter 23

Tuesday evening after their supper of pizochels, when Dominik, Alfons, and Barla had left the table, Clementina sat with her parents and Catrina.

"I'm going to leave," Clementina said firmly, without introduction.

Her parents both looked up at her in surprise. Catrina kept looking down at the table, as if she had felt this coming.

"What, Tina?" asked her father.

"I said I am going to leave. I cannot stay here in the village."

No one had spoken of Gion or of his marriage since the wedding day, but they all knew what she meant.

Signora Cavaziel stood up calmly and started clearing the dishes, replying, "Of course it is difficult for you now. We understand, Papa and I." She shot him a glance, willing him to understand and agree. "I think it would do you good to go away for a little while."

"Not for a little while, Mumma. I'm going to leave for good, for always."

"What?!" Her mother dropped back into her seat again, clanking the stack of plates still in her hands. Her eyes were wide and she looked at her husband, expecting him to explain. He looked as startled as she did.

"They will be back from their honeymoon in two more weeks, and I want to be gone by then."

Clementina looked at Catrina for support, but her sister only stared at the table, looking like she was fighting back tears. Clementina felt her own tears forming, but she fought them back.

"To Chur, then?" asked her father. "Or Zürich? We could ask your cousin, Primus, to help her there," he said, looking worriedly at his wife.

"No, not Zürich," answered Clementina quietly. "I have decided. I will go to America." She said it firmly, with more determination than she felt. She might as well have been telling them that she was going to the moon.

"Jesus Maria!" cried her mother, closing her eyes and crossing herself before sinking her head to her hands. Her father just stared at her, dumbfounded.

"America, Tina!" he finally said, still staring.

Her mother recovered enough to speak. "What are you thinking, daughter? You can't go to America! It is so far away! We don't know anyone in America! You don't speak American! You will get over him, and there will be someone else. You don't have to go so far away! Go to Zürich."

"You don't understand, Mumma. I cannot stay. I want to go far, far away, to start over. I *have* to go."

Catrina's head jerked up at this, and in her eyes Clementina caught what might be a flicker of understanding.

Maybe she guessed the reason for Clementina's determination. But she bit her bottom lip and said nothing.

Seeing her parents so distraught grieved her, but she was willing to brave the current sorrow now to avoid what would only mean greater shame and anguish for them. Clementina took a deep breath.

"I have thought it all out. I have a little money saved from what Tante Lucrezia has given me for my birthdays and from the berries we've sold in the summer. I was saving it for my trousseau, but..." Here she stopped for a moment to compose herself, and then continued pragmatically, "well, now this will be a better use for it. I have all the linens that I've made, and I haven't yet embroidered my initials on. I can sell them. Signora Baptista has always liked my embroidery. She once said she could sell things for me in Chur. I will take them to her tomorrow. It is not a lot, but I think it will be enough."

She stopped and finally looked at her parents. They simply looked back at her, too astonished and brokenhearted to say a word.

***

In the end, the amount Clementina was able to scrape together would not have been enough. But when, after a few half-hearted tries to change her mind—or at least to convince her go somewhere closer—her parents admitted that her resolve was unbending, and they each came to her separately.

"Here is almost fifty francs," said her mother one evening, carefully placing the bills on the table where

Clementina was seated, finishing an embroidery piece for Signora Baptista. She said the words casually, as if holding so much money at one time were a common occurrence. Clementina's eyes grew round at the sight of the wealth in front of her.

"Mama! How did you...? Mama, I can't take all that!"

"Shhh, child," her mother answered, standing next to the chair and pulling her eldest against her chest and stroking her hair.

"It was for a rainy day, and I suppose that day has come."

"But Mama!"

"Shhh, daughter! Don't say another word," she answered, her voice breaking. Clementina was quiet and rested her head against her mother. She could hear her heartbeat, and she felt her mother's stifled sobs.

The next morning, her father found her when she was out feeding the chickens in the courtyard behind the house.

"Ah, little Tina," he said, pushing back his wide-brimmed work hat. "Will you take a hen with you? Then you could have eggs on the steamship and everyone else would know that the Swiss truly are backward mountain people. You will have a reputation to keep up!"

Clementina laughed as he had intended her to. She knew he was trying hard to keep his own spirits up.

"I came out to give you this. Maybe don't mention it to your mother." He pushed a small envelope into her apron pocket. She looked at him questioningly. In answer, he only reached around her neck with his left arm, and pulling her quickly to him, kissed her on the forehead. Then he turned, and straightening his hat again, he stomped off down the road swinging his ax and whistling loudly.

Even Catrina gave her a little bit of savings from the berries they had sold in the summers. When Clementina protested this latest bit of generosity, Catrina only said coyly, "When you are a rich American you can send me a new hat to pay me back."

Realistically, she knew she would need all the money she could get, even though she hated taking it from her family who had so little to begin with. Just getting there would use up almost all that she had. She would have to find work almost immediately.

But as she went quietly around the village to say her goodbyes, she had a stroke of luck, or providence, as her mother called it. Signora Candinas was a young mother who Clementina had always liked and admired. She had eight children, all very close in age, and was usually wearing one on her hip. But as busy as she was, she always had a kind word for others, and especially for the village girls.

"My cousin, Beatrice, in St. Gallen, had a friend who went to America. She stayed at a Benedictine convent in New York City until she went west to Ohio."

Signora Cavaziel was overjoyed at the news and insisted on writing the convent immediately. Clementina let her, though she wondered if the letter would arrive much before her. It helped her mother to be able to do something active for her daughter. She had also helped her write to the agent in Chur who was representing *Norddeutscher Lloyd*—the steamship company advertising emigration in the local Romantsch newspaper–to purchase her ticket.

Her ship would sail Monday the 30th of September. Saturday morning, she walked with all her family to the train station. She had already said her goodbyes to each individually and there was not much left to say. Nobody said much of anything and her mother looked stunned and in shock, as if until this moment she hadn't really believed Clementina would go through with it. Her brothers seemed jealous of her going to America, but touchingly anxious for her safety. Alfons pushed something small into her hands. It was a tiny wooden goat he had carved, no taller than her thumb. She kissed him on his forehead. Catrina blinked away tears as she embraced her sister one last time.

Then the little red train whooshed down the valley from the direction of Disentis, whistled as it rounded the bend past their home, past the church and into the station. Three minutes later, it chugged out again with Clementina on board, following the waters of the Rhine as they poured down the valley, out of the mountains, past the small towns of Switzerland, out onto the plains of Europe, past the cities and on out to the sea.

Chapter 24

"Can you imagine? I had hardly ever been farther than two hours away from home in my life, but I took the train to Chur, to Zürich, then to Paris, and then to Le Havre. I was terrified, but determined. But all during that long train ride I wondered if I was doing the right thing. The one thing that kept me going was that now I had spent my money and I had no choice.

"I was terribly sick all the way across the Atlantic. What was seasickness and what morning sickness I couldn't tell. A French girl was travelling across too, and she was kind and brought me broth and crackers when I was too ill to get to the third-class dining hall.

"When we got to New York, I went to the Sisters of Divine Providence. It was the convent of St. Benedict on the Lower East Side that Signora Candinas had told me about. It was a mission for young Catholic girls arriving in the city. So many were arriving, unable to communicate and without any notion of how to get by and ending up in very bad situations. The nuns had only received my mother's letter the week before, but they welcomed me so kindly. Some spoke a little German so I was able to communicate. One of the nuns was so loving and understanding that I eventually told her my whole story. The first person and the last person until now.

"I had thought a lot on the voyage over, and I knew I would need help. I couldn't hide my pregnancy forever. That sister helped me more than I could ever repay, not that she would have wanted that. But she seemed so truly to understand how I felt, that later I wondered what her own story was. Perhaps she had had an experience a little like mine.

"Anyway, she helped me find work doing piecework and sewing collars and cuffs for one of the clothing manufacturers in the city. I worked through the fall, winter, and spring and stayed on at the convent.

"At first the noise of the city deafened me. I used to lie awake at night in the dormitory room and try to distinguish one sound from another in the din—a faraway car horn, truck engines, construction work, people shouting—but it was impossible. They all blended together in the sound of an enormous busy city. It astounded me that so much could be happening in the middle of the night! The sisters encouraged us to take walks in our spare time to learn our way around the city. I was overwhelmed at first—so many people, so many buildings, so much dirt. But sometimes, when I walked in Midtown and looked up and down the long avenues with the skyscrapers thousands of feet high on either side, they seemed almost familiar. They reminded me of my long valley at home with the mountains rising above us. It was only much later that I heard people talk about the Canyons of New York and the Mountains of Manhattan.

"Sister Felicity arranged things for the baby's arrival, and then she helped arrange an adoption with a well-to-do childless couple in Boston. On June 10th, I had a baby girl, just as the roses were coming into bloom. There was a climbing rose growing on the convent wall, and when I left for the hospital the flowers were still in bud. When I came back a few days later, the wall was covered with pink blossoms.

"Giving up my daughter was the hardest thing I have ever had to do, much harder than leaving my home. I loved her. But she was safe now, I knew, with a good, secure family. She would be far better off than I was, who had nothing and now had to find work in a world entering the Great Depression. Can you imagine it? The stock market crash on Black Tuesday was three weeks after my arrival. If I had understood what it meant, I would have been terrified, but all that was too great and mighty for me. I just hoped that I could make enough to provide my own clothes and help a little with the food at the convent.

"After my baby was born, the sisters found me a place as a governess and seamstress for the McAllister family. Somehow the word 'Swiss' made people sit up and take notice. They assumed you were sensible and very organized, just the qualities wanted in a governess. The McAllisters were a kind family and quite wealthy. But they never quite grasped that my name was Clementina and not Clementine. Eventually I stopped correcting them—they were used to having their way—and a way it was fitting, a new name for a new country. I was very comfortable there and I stayed with them for many years. I worked, caring for other people's children, but always thinking privately about my own, growing up somewhere out there in the world. She was lost to me, I knew, but she was somewhere here in this country, so somehow I was tied here as well. I couldn't go back home.

"Eventually the McAllister children grew up, and then I was a seamstress in another family. They were not as agreeable, and after a few years there, I had saved up a good enough amount of money and had enough extra clients that I decided that with careful planning, I could make it out on my own. So I moved here, and here I have been ever since. I've gotten very used to the city now, but it is a long, long way from my mountain village.

"So you see, Helen, I never wanted to be what you call a 'career woman.' I didn't want to be 'modern.' Have I enjoyed my life here? Yes. Is it what I had wanted? No. I just wanted to be a mother, to make a home for a man I loved, to raise my own children.

"What you had, what you've given up—a life of simple domesticity—many people wish for, would give anything for. I am afraid I don't feel sorry for you. Or at least not much. I feel sorry for the husband who is left behind, probably young and confused, like my Gion. But at least he is still waiting for you. And I am glad for your sake that you have no children."

The room was still for many minutes, dust particles floating lazily in the low rays of afternoon sun that were somehow finding their way through the apartment buildings outside and through the window. Helen sat quiet and pensive, so wrapped up in Clementine's story that she hardly heard the rebuke at the end of it. Clementine gazed down at her hands, her face weary. Then she took a deep breath, and made a move to rise.

"So you never went back to Switzerland?" asked Helen suddenly, not wanting the story to end.

Clementine sat back in her chair.

"Once. My father became ill and then passed away four years ago. I stayed with my sister, Catrina. In the end, it was she who married and stayed in the village—she who always wanted to travel. Her daughter, Maria, is nine years old. She writes me letters regularly. I think she was quite impressed with her 'American' auntie who wears red lipstick." She smiled.

"And Gion? Did you see him again? Didn't you ever want to tell him the truth?"

Clementine turned and gazed out the window.

"I thought of telling him before I left the first time. And then I thought maybe I would write a letter after the baby was born, but I didn't have the courage. When I went home for Papa's funeral, I thought maybe I could be brave enough, so many years later. Instead, I found out he had died in an avalanche the previous winter. No one had told me; they didn't want to stir up old memories and old feelings. They had no idea that they are always with me."

"What about your baby? Did you ever learn anything more? What happened to her?"

"Sister Felicity didn't tell me much, and at the time I didn't really want to know too much. I think she knew that would only make it harder. I know she went to Boston. But not a day has passed that I haven't thought of her, what she might be like now. Would she look like me? Or like her father? Not a day has passed that I haven't prayed for her, that God would protect her and be as kind to her as He has been to me."

"*Kind* to you?"

"Yes, kind. God is kind. He has always been kind." She stopped and sighed. "For a long time I was sad. Then I was angry at life. Now I think I have learned better. Despite my judgment and my mistakes, I have had a good life. I have work that I enjoy, people that appreciate me, and interesting people to meet." Clementine looked at Helen as she said this, and raised her eyebrows, smiling. "Should we really ask for much more? Isn't it enough?

"But now you should probably go, Helen. I am quite tired, and maybe you are, too."

Helen was indeed tired. The long afternoon inside someone else's life had exhausted her. As she rose to go and thanked her hostess, her mind still swirled with the details of the story, and she tried to remember why she had gone to see Clementine in the first place. What had she been so upset about? When she recalled Vladimir, she blushed with embarrassment at herself. Now it seemed so incredibly petty.

On the bus up Madison rode a young nanny and her two small charges. They were brothers, dressed in matching sailor suits and as they argued over lollipops, their nanny corrected them kindly but wearily. With the boys quiet again, the young woman turned and gazed out of the window at the passing apartment houses. *What was that girl's story?* Helen wondered. She'd never wondered before. Nannies were a part of the landscape of New York City, like bankers and hot dog sellers. She'd never before imagined any of them having a story. But not long ago, one of them had been Clementine, with a lost baby and a broken heart, whose story had nearly made Helen weep. *Did everyone have a story like that?* she wondered.

Chapter 25

Maybe it was just because it was November—a time of shorter days and pensive thoughts—but over the next few weeks, Helen could not shake Clementine's story from her mind. There was nothing to distract her. The weather was bad. Vladimir had disappeared into government custody, and everyone in the office pretended he had never been there. Helen did the same and was surprised to find how easy it was. Even the news on Wednesday the fourteenth that Soviet troops had succeeded in effectively stamping out the resistance movement in Budapest did not bring that particularly exciting rush of feelings at the tragic misfortune of others. That the Hungarian Revolution that had been so promising was no more seemed only an inevitable fact of the general gloominess.

As November drizzle descended on New York City's short days and long chilly nights, Helen's thoughts of handsome cosmopolitan agents and her important part in a democratic free press were replaced by images of a solitary Swiss village girl, simply dressed, leaving on a train, boarding a ship across the dark sea, leaving, forever leaving. When Helen looked down Madison Avenue from her seat on the bus, she saw the long Alpine valley Clementine had described and found herself missing the mountains she had never seen. When clouds hid the tops of the skyscrapers, she wondered how the mountains looked now, their peaks hidden by mist like the top of the Chrysler building.

She took to daydreaming about the nannies that she now saw everywhere, imagining exotic origins and romantically sad stories for them as they shuffled their charges around. Until, of course, one would open her mouth and betray by her accent that she did, in fact, hail from Brooklyn. *But they could still have a story, couldn't they?* thought Helen. Even if they only came from Brooklyn? That girl with the red hair cut in a bob, for instance; maybe, just maybe, she'd been cast from the family home because she refused to marry the homely heir to a necktie factory!

Helen finally succeeded in planning a German lesson with Thomas Lawson. He came one evening with his grammar texts and tomes in old German print. But either he quickly realized that Helen's German was more picked up in the bakeries and sausage shops of Munich than learned from a textbook—she was even more uncertain about the irregular verbs than he was—or he surmised as much from her look of dismay upon seeing his books. So instead of boring German verb endings, they spent a happy hour discussing the most recent gloomy news from Hungary. Thomas seemed pleased to talk with a woman unafraid to discuss world affairs. And when Helen did finally reveal how he'd been right about Vladimir being a spy, Thomas—though surprised at being correct—didn’t gloat in the slightest, but rather was concerned about her well-being in the ensuing bureaucratic kafuffle. He was also interested in her new friendship with Clementine and Romantsch, and he asked all kinds of questions about the language that she couldn’t really answer. Rose made spaghetti for them all, Thomas stayed for dinner, and he finally left much later than originally planned. He really was an awfully nice man, Helen thought when he departed. Too bad he wasn’t at all the kind she was interested in.

***

For Thanksgiving, Rose's parents invited Helen to their home in Bridgewater. It was a huge house, built of large gray stone, and despite her own aspirations for wealth and decorum, Helen felt intimidated as they drove around the large circular drive. But the Whitakers were very kind and welcoming. They were both tall and fair and reserved, but despite their quiet manner, they both went out of their way to put Helen at ease.

"You've no idea how glad we are that you and Rose found each other, and we're delighted to finally meet you," smiled Mrs. Whitaker as she led Helen through the massive front door. "George was quite worried when she told us she'd found a roommate in the classifieds! But Rose can be very determined," she said with an affectionate glance at her daughter, "and she usually has good instincts." She put her hand gently on Helen's shoulder and smiled warmly at her. "In this case, she certainly did."

The long weekend was peaceful and elegant. Helen was intrigued to learn more about Rose as she watched her in her natural surroundings. Despite the efforts Rose made to live life on her own terms, she clearly adored her parents and they doted on her. Mr. Whitaker was exactly how Helen expected a university professor to be. He wore tweed coats and muttered to himself as he walked through the house. It startled her at first, thinking he was speaking to her.

"I beg your pardon, sir?" she asked politely.

"What? What??" he asked with wildly raised eyebrows. "Oh, no, never mind me," he said with a smile. "I talk to myself is all. Alice stopped minding me years ago and now she doesn't pay attention to anything I say," he added with a twinkle in his eye. "Do you, Alice?" he asked his wife who had just come into the living room with a bouquet of the last of her garden's chrysanthemums.

Mrs. Whitaker raised her head vaguely in their direction, but went on arranging the flowers on the antique writing desk that stood to the side of the stone fireplace.

"There now, you see?" asked Mr. Whitaker roguishly.

The holiday meal was as traditional as the turkey in Norman Rockwell's painting. Mrs. Whitaker busied Rose and Helen in the kitchen, peeling potatoes and slicing yams, while she prepared the turkey to go in the oven.

"It's the cooperative effort I love about Thanksgiving," she said. "Everybody helps out with what they know how to do best."

"And apparently, what I do best is peel potatoes," muttered Rose, "I've been perfecting my method for over twenty years!"

Helen smiled, but thought to herself that she was glad she could help out. What she knew how to do best was slice things, like these yams. Despite her mother being a home economics teacher, Helen had never learned much cooking at home. It was a case of the shoemaker's children going barefoot, she supposed. She had never really wanted to learn, and when her mother arrived home after school, she was happy to have her kitchen to herself and not to bother teaching anyone else. Still, in retrospect, knowing how to cook a few meals might have helped things with Heinrich. Men were such a bundle of appetites, and perhaps it was unreasonable to expect them to be nice when they hadn't been properly fed.

"It's a good thing Eunice is bringing the pies, we wouldn't have time nor space in the oven. I tried again to get Aunt Martha to come, but getting her out of the city is like getting a pearl out of an oyster. But she had plenty of plans for the day, she said. I think she and her friends just sit and play poker around the turkey."

Aunt Eunice, Mr. Whitaker's older sister, arrived with Uncle Richard and their children and grandchildren. The big house resounded with noise and laughter and games that contrasted with the quiet Helen heard when she telephoned her parents at Mrs. Whitaker's insistence.

"Don't worry, dear, don't think of the expense. You won't talk for hours and it's important, it's a holiday. Thank your mother for sharing you with us."

Her father answered the telephone, and even though the line hummed with static, the clear sound of his measured, baritone voice across the miles filled her with an ache that made her voice catch.

"Daddy?"

Chapter 26

After Thanksgiving, Helen returned to the city buoyed up with the feeling of peace and prevailing domestic contentment of the Whitakers' home. The Christmas season sparkled ahead with a million lights and possibilities like a field of snow under the stars. She felt rested and ready for it, and she began again to entertain thoughts of soirées with debonair cosmopolitans and to make a mental list of those in her acquaintance that might be suitable. But her peace shattered abruptly just as she began to enter wholeheartedly into the festivities.

One Saturday, two weeks before Christmas, she came home from an afternoon of shopping to a Western Union telegram. A pang of worry for her parents struck her, and as soon as she walked into the apartment, she plopped down her bags in the hallway, threw her coat on the back of the sofa, and opened it. It was from Heinrich. She nodded absently to Rose's friendly greeting and sat down heavily.

TO HELEN HARTMANN
MOTOR ACCIDENT AND SIEGFRIED KILLED STOP MUTTI BESIDE HERSELF STOP WILL WRITE DIRECTLY STOP
HEINRICH

"Helen, what's wrong?!" demanded Rose, looking at Helen's pale face.

"It's from Heinrich, my...husband. His brother's been killed." She looked up quickly at Rose to see if her frank admission of a husband had shocked her. If it did, she didn't show it. Somehow, to Rose, she couldn't sugarcoat the truth. He was still her husband, legally.

"He's still in Munich, isn't he?" Rose didn't seem surprised at all.

"Yes, and his brother Siegfried, too, and their mother. Siegfried is so young, just finishing university. And their mother, she's already been through so much. Their father was in the German army and died on the Russian front." She held up the telegram to Rose who had crossed the room to her. She sat next to Helen and read the letter, the reflection of the lamp on her tortoise shell glasses hiding her expression. Then she took a deep breath and turned to her friend.

"I am so sorry, Helen. How can I help you? Shall we cable anyone? Should we send flowers?"

"Oh, yes. I don't even know what to think. Yes, flowers would be wonderful."

Once again, Helen let Rose take care of her. Rose made her a cup of tea and then called around to a florist to see about international deliveries. In the end, they drafted a telegram to a friend in the Munich Committee office to ask about sending flowers to Heinrich's mother. It seemed the most sensitive thing to do.

Helen spent the next few days wondering how she should feel. She felt sorrow, of course. She had liked Siegfried very much, and he had often been the carefree antithesis to Heinrich's seriousness. But although Rose seemed to consider the whole affair with great gravity, Helen somehow couldn't. She couldn't quite feel that this was still the brother of her husband. They weren't *really* still married, after all, she told herself. Siegfried was not *really* any longer part of her family.

Three days later came a letter by express. An enclosed newspaper clipping showed a horrible photo of the accident site with the headline: *Zwei junge Münchner vom Lastzug überfahren, Two Munich Youths Run Over by Delivery Truck*. The enclosed letter was written on onion skin paper in Heinrich's sprawling hand.

Dear Helen,

I am writing this letter with a feeling that is indescribable. Siegfried is dead, and suddenly one realizes all the things one missed doing with him. And there is Mutti who doesn't yet believe what has happened. She needs a lot of consolation, and I am trying very hard to give that to her. I am surprised I can give her as much as I do. I have the feeling of a crazy driving emptiness, realizing that my relationship to Mutti and Siegfried had always been kind of loose and that I have now lost a great chance to change that.

It happened yesterday morning. A couple of months ago I had bought a motor scooter from Kurt from my office. Siegfried had taken it sometimes when I was away, I guess. Mutti and I forbade him to do so, but you know how these boys are. Yesterday morning I was still sleeping, and he took the Vespa again. Maybe he knew that I sleep late on Saturdays and wanted to be back in time. To Mutti he said that he would go to lectures at the Polytechnikum and then to a friend's to do homework. Instead, as we now know, he went right to his friend Karli's, and later went on toward Landshut (about 40 km from here) where Karli's grandmother lives. Karli's briefcase contained dirty washing and that indicates that they were going to Karli's Oma. Near Freising, halfway to Landshut, the scooter slipped in a curve, both fell right under a truck which came on the opposite side. Both were killed instantly. Skull and backbone fractures. People say that Karli was driving. I never saw him driving, and I guess that Siegfried wanted to do him a favor.

I went to the scene immediately. It was terrible. Siegfried's body is deformed, his head scratched and fractured. If only I knew how to make Mutti understand that she can't see him anymore. Mutti is so down that I fear for her mind. I had the doctor here yesterday who gave her things to calm down. I don't know yet how everything will go on, but somehow it must go on. Maybe I can persuade Mutti to visit somewhere and be away from Munich for awhile. The burial will be on Tuesday or Wednesday. Karli's parents are still in Leipzig. It will be a great shock, since he was the only child. For Siegfried, it is double hard, since his studies started to be very satisfying. From January on he would have received a scholarship of 150 marks a month.

I am telling you all this because I have to talk to somebody. Perhaps you will understand, and maybe you will also understand that our own problems will now have to be postponed a little.

I understand Siegfried wrote to you a few days ago. He liked you very much. Also Mutti is very fond of you. Her first thought was you and that we should send you a cable. I miss you more than ever.

Much love,

Heinrich

Helen read the letter with her stomach in knots and her heart twisted up inside her. She felt sick. In her mind she saw Heinrich writing this letter, alone in their apartment, with no friends to console him, with a mother half-crazed with grief, and his only brother now gone forever. His words were so tender, so sad that it took her breath away. He had almost never been so genuine with her, so honest about what he felt. And his parting words, they were an appeal. She could not deny it. He wanted her. He needed her. He was asking her to come back to him.

For the first time in a long time, she remembered all that had been good about Munich and her life there. She thought of Mutti, and how kind and welcoming she had been to Helen. She recalled when she had first arrived and didn't yet speak much German, how Mutti had told Heinrich to tell her in English how glad she was to have another woman in the family. She had insisted, in fact, that Helen call her "Mutti," Mama. In the first long first months after her arrival, while Heinrich was at work, Helen would go for afternoon coffee in Mutti's small, neat apartment while the older woman patiently told her the German words for everything on the table. Fork: *Gabel*, spoon: *Löffel*. Helen repeated the words and laughed at herself. What they couldn't say with words, they shared with smiles and nods. But Helen did learn slowly. And then one afternoon Mutti picked up a picture from the bookcase and brought it to Helen.

"Do you recognize them?" Mutti asked slowly with a smile. Helen had now learned enough German to understand. It was a wedding photo. In it Helen stood next to Heinrich, her tea-length white satin skirt flaring out, covering the legs of his rented tuxedo. Their posed smiles were fixed on their young faces. They held hands, but stood slightly apart from each other, looking out at the camera, side by side like the two strangers that they were.

"Heinrich sent me this photograph after your wedding last January. I was still up in Northern Germany then, in the part occupied by the Soviets. We were still living as displaced persons. Siegfried had already moved to Munich to go to university. It was getting harder and harder to leave the Soviet sector. So when the picture arrived, I packed up and went to Berlin, where we could still get from East Berlin to West Berlin and then on to West Germany. For the most part, they were only letting younger people leave to go to the west, like Siegfried and Heinrich. But I took this picture and went to the authorities. 'Look,' I said, 'my son has married an American woman. The Soviets will not like this if they find out, and I will be in danger. You will have to let me across.' And they did. Thank heavens!" She smiled at Helen and cupped her daughter-in-law's face in her hand. "You were sent by God. It was so hard to lose Ernst, but now with you here, we are a family again."

At the time, Helen's heart had felt so warm, so filled with joy that she could have played a role of benefit in the life of this kind woman. She had been glad, then, to be a part of a family. It was only later that she had grown increasingly weary of what Heinrich's Germanic idea of family seemed to be. She had wondered what Heinrich's father had been like. Had *he* been so traditional and demanding of his wife? Or had Heinrich become that way because he hadn't had a father to emulate? It had struck her many times in those days, walking around Munich, how few older men there were. The fathers were all gone, killed in the war.

Now, three years later, Helen's heart felt a piercing pang of conscience. Gertrud Hartmann had lost first her husband, then her daughter-in-law, now her son. In one of the first letters Heinrich had written to Helen after she left, he had told her that he had tried to explain to Mutti, but she couldn't understand. Why had Helen left? When was she coming back? Helen had never even tried to explain it to Mutti herself. Now she was asking the same kinds of questions about Siegfried. No wonder Heinrich feared for her mental health.

I could go back, she thought. *It wouldn't fix everything, but it would help.*

The thought had jumped into her mind before she'd had a chance to control it. It was unthinkable. She couldn't go back! She had crossed that bridge and burned it. She had remade her life here. She didn't want to be a German housewife. She wanted freedom and independence.

But it would be the right thing to do.

I don't want to do the right thing!

Helen's thoughts startled her. She tried in vain to quell the two voices clamoring inside her mind.

It would be hard; that's why you don't want to.

I don't have to, and no one can make me! I won't go! I'm sorry for Mutti and for Heinrich, but their problems are no longer mine.

Even as she listened to the two voices doing battle in her mind, Helen felt like she was listening to a three-year-old, like one of the tiresome unruly children she watched on the bus. She saw how selfish her thoughts were, and it appalled her. Even so, she determined not to change her mind. She sat on the sofa, clutched one of the green silk throw cushions to her chest and read the letter again, half hoping it would contain different news. Rose found her there when she walked in twenty minutes later with a bag of groceries.

"What is it, Helen?" she asked as soon as she saw her roommate's face. She quickly went to dump the grocery bag in the kitchen and then came back and sat down on the sofa, ready to listen. *Dear Rose*, thought Helen, *always so ready to be compassionate.* It was as if somehow Rose knew, and didn't mind, that she was forever to be a supporting actress in someone else's play. If she were any less narcissistic, Helen might well have been embarrassed that nearly all of their interactions revolved around her. As it was, grateful for the attention, she poured out her heart and the contents of the letter to Rose's listening ears.

"He wants me to come back!" she cried at the end. "I *can't* go back!" There was a pause and her words hung in the air.

"Oh, can't you?" replied Rose unexpectedly. "Why not? And why wouldn't you, Helen?" she said, turning to gaze at her. The look on her face was enigmatic. "I guess I figured you'd had some sort of heartbreak, but frankly, the way you've acted, I assumed it was all over with. But as long as you are still married, isn't it your duty? Listen to his words, Helen! Don't you have any compassion for the man?" The look on her face was incredulous, and the words were not anything that Helen had expected to hear.

"Was he cruel? Was he unfaithful? Did he beat you? Did he not provide enough for you?" She paused, but her pale green eyes stared into Helen's. "Or was it just that he didn't make every situation about you? Did he just not give in to your every whim?"

Helen felt her breath coming faster and faster and her cheeks growing hot, but she was quiet. She could not think of anything to say. But she felt anger starting to grow.

Rose spoke again, more slowly.

"Helen, the poor man just lost his brother, and his mother is losing her mind." She reached out and took Helen's hand. "Think, Helen, and don't just react. Have compassion and think beyond what *you* feel." Helen didn't know whether to cry or yell in anger.

Then Rose stood abruptly. "I'm going back out," she said a little too loudly. "The second grade teacher, Miss Edman, got free tickets to that musical *My Fair Lady* from her brother who's the lighting tech." With that, she went to put her groceries away and then disappeared into the bedroom to dress. They had never had a discussion like that before. She had never heard *Rose* speak like that before. Helen stayed where she was for a long time, then warmed some soup for supper and went to bed early. She lay in the dark and thought about it all over again, Rose's words stinging her ears even more than her tears stung her eyes.

Chapter 27

Helen went to see Clementine early the next week, ostensibly bringing a box of chocolates for Christmas. If she hoped for a different response from that of Rose, she was mistaken. The older lady was warm and pleasant, but when she heard Helen's news, she was not shy to voice her opinion.

"Since you ask me, I will tell you that since you are still married legally, I think it is your duty to be with him. You made a promise to be with him in good times and in bad, didn't you? What is a bad time, if not this?"

"I *can't* go," Helen began. "It's not as if we're *really* married anymore. We're not together. And even when we were together, we weren't."

"But only because you left. He has not yet given up on you. This letter shows it."

"He could have followed me!" said Helen savagely. "He could have shown me how much he wanted me, if he didn't want to give me up. I guess he didn't try that hard."

"That is a silly, romantic notion. It's worthy of a sixteen-year-old girl, not a grown woman."

"I…" Helen began.

"Helen," Clementine interrupted her, "did you ever really love him? Or did you only love the idea of him?"

The question stopped Helen's protest short.

"You loved the idea of a foreign husband, didn't you? Did you love what you imagined your life would be? Did you dream it would be all romance and traveling and no ordinariness? Or did you ever just love him as a person? You should have known better than to come to me if you wanted help to forget your conscience. You have someone who wants you, who is asking for you. That is enormous."

Helen departed before long, politely thanking Clementine for her thoughts, showing an exterior as calm and collected as ever, while inside her thoughts were all in a jumble. Back and forth her mind ranged over her dilemma, and she was only too relieved with the arrival of Christmas and the excuse not to think about it all for awhile. Rose never brought up the topic again, though she looked once or twice like she might broach the subject.

On Christmas morning Helen allowed herself the extravagant expense of a telephone call to her parents, and in the afternoon she joined Rose's family again for dinner. The office was closed between December 25th and January 1st, but there was Mr. and Mrs. Major's Christmas party to attend, as well as cocktail parties put on by various emigré groups working with The Committee. Then one had to recover from it all, and at the same time, work began again and with it a flurry of Mr. Major's new projects.

Somehow, nearly a month had passed quickly by since she had received Heinrich's telegram. When she realized it one day looking at her agenda, she knew that even she could not wait any longer. In decency, he deserved an answer. She would have to make a decision. And as she contemplated this, she realized to her surprise that despite the busyness of the last few weeks, her decision had already been made.

All through the holidays, while she flitted from party to party, thoughts of Clementine would slip through her mind. Clementine who left what was comfortable and known for the sake of a greater purpose. That kind of sacrifice inspired her, and made her want to do the same. Fighting Communism was inspiring too, especially during a crisis like the one in Hungary. But she had to admit to herself that honestly, fighting Communism by typing and re-typing memos was becoming a little dull; the whole thing was taking so long. She wished the Communists would just realize the inevitable and give up.

On the other hand, 1957 was new and full of hope. Surely things would be different now that Heinrich appreciated her, that he truly appreciated what he had lost. Suddenly one morning, her resolve was clear. She would go. She would bring healing and comfort to poor, dear Heinrich and his mother. And truly, her happiness would not matter to her, as long as she could make others happy! How pleased Rose would be and Clementine, too, when she told them. She imagined their nodding looks of sympathetic approval. The thought fairly thrilled her.

So with her mind made up and a few more days to solidify her plans, she cabled Heinrich her intentions of returning. While she waited for his answer, she shyly told

Rose her plans one evening. Her response was not the one expected. Rose looked surprised.

"What?" cried Helen, "Isn't that what you thought I should do?"

"Well, in a way, yes. But Helen, it's been over a month since he wrote you."

"I know, it took me a while to sort it all out. But now I have, and I'm going back."

"Alright," said Rose doubtfully. "What did he say?"

"I haven't heard back yet, I've only just cabled."

Apart from the vague air of skepticism, which annoyed Helen, Rose became very friendly that week. She seemed sorry to be losing her roommate, but offered to help with travel plans or packing when necessary. Rose was so practical; Helen hadn't really thought about travel plans. She could take a jet plane like she had the last time, but the ship was so much more economical, an important consideration in her budget.

Chapter 28

That week while she awaited a reply, Thomas came to visit.

"I thought I'd drop by and see how your holidays were, and how 1957 is treating you so far," he said when they were comfortably installed with a glass of sherry for each.

He had spent his university vacation back home with his family, and Helen hadn't seen him for over a month. And in that time so much had seemed to change in her life. Helen didn't quite know how to broach the subject. Thomas was just a casual friend; she didn't owe him any explanations, yet somehow she felt awkward. Maybe the best way was the most direct.

She took a large sip of her drink and blurted out, "I'm going back to Munich. I'm actually married. Still…married." Thomas stared at her blankly, and she continued awkwardly. "I mean, I thought it was all over. It seemed to be all over, but my...husband's brother died recently and he needs me. So I've decided to go back. He's why I lived in Munich in the first place."

Thomas said nothing, but he sat up a little straighter in his arm chair. He looked away from her and down at the floor. He opened his mouth and then shut it again. Helen felt her face flush crimson, and was annoyed at it.

"I'm sorry…I know…I know we're friends, and I should have mentioned it before…but, there just never seemed to be the right moment. It didn't seem necessary."

Thomas' manner took on a new layer of formality.

"Thank you for saying. But you know, you don't owe me anything."

Helen nodded half-heartedly and gave a weak smile. She knew she didn't owe him anything. Why did it feel like she wanted to give him an explanation? Why did she want him to understand? Thomas seemed to be at a loss for what to say. For once, Helen didn't feel like filling the silence.

Finally he spoke slowly. "When will you be leaving?"

"I'm not quite sure, really. As soon as I hear back from Heinrich I'll make my arrangements. In the next few weeks, I imagine."

"Hmm," he said looking down, apparently lost in thought.

"Thomas," Helen began.

He looked up at her pensively.

"You've been sweet to me. A good friend, better than I deserve. Thank you."

He took in her words.

"Well then, I wish you all the best, Helen. Dear Helen." He looked at her almost tenderly as he said the last words, slowly and with meaning. And then he stood up suddenly, the tender look gone, and in its place was his sunny smile. His manner changed to his usual joviality.

"It has been the greatest pleasure knowing you," he said gallantly. "Perhaps one day our paths will cross again. Now it is time for me to be going."

He walked to the door. She followed and as he stood at the open doorway, he turned and swept her hand up to his lips, as he had when she'd met him that first day in September. Then he was gone. Helen stood in the doorway a long time, her insides feeling odd, recalling the tender look he had let her see for just a moment. She had seen many looks from men directed at her, but not yet that one.

Chapter 29

By the week's end, Helen still hadn't heard from Heinrich. She cabled again, repeating her message of before.

DEAR HEINRICH

COMING BACK STOP DEBATING SHIP OR PLANE STOP PLEASE ADVISE STOP

She waited another few short February days and then one evening came home to a return telegram. Ripping it open she read.

DEAR HELEN

DON'T TROUBLE YOURSELF STOP

MUTTI AND I MUDDLED THROUGH AS WE COULD AND DOING BETTER STOP YOUR INTEREST IN OUR WELL-BEING HAS BEEN LATE IN COMING STOP

YOU SHOULD STAY IN NEW YORK I WILL SIGN AND RETURN DIVORCE PAPERS YOU SENT LAST SUMMER STOP

WISHING YOU HEALTH AND FUTURE HAPPINESS

HEINRICH

Helen's hands began to shake. She had never imagined a response like this! She felt cold, then very hot. Walking to the window, she opened it and let the cool air in. Outside the gray drizzle of a late February afternoon was falling. She read through the short letter again. Heinrich's words were so cold! They felt like a hard slap across her cheek.

All the planning and agitation of the past two weeks ground to a halt like the sound on Rose's phonograph when the power inadvertently switched off. What was she going to do now? For a few weeks she had had such purpose, such confidence that she was doing the right thing. She had never allowed herself the possibility that she would not be wanted. She had not yet announced her departure at work, but with bittersweet feelings she had imagined the looks on the faces of Pansy and Mr. Major when they realized all that she was laying on the altar of self-sacrifice. Now, with a start, she realized how glad she was she hadn't said anything or she'd be out of a job. No doubt Pansy would have already been wheedling her way into Helen's desk and position.

She quickly sent another telegram with a half-hearted appeal, but the answer came back even faster and colder than before.

PLEASE STAY IN NEW YORK STOP

The worst was having to tell her friends that she had failed. Rose said simply, "Well, at least you tried," but beyond that didn't say much at all. Surprisingly, Thomas did not seem sorry at her sad story either, but instead grew very quiet.

"I've been going back to church lately," he said abruptly. "I've never been much of a churchgoer, more of a doubter actually, but I thought it might help me gain some perspective. Do you want to come along? Maybe it could do the same for you."

Chapter 30

Helen sat on the hard wooden pew next to Thomas in a large airy sanctuary on East 91st. The pews were old and worn shiny from years of countless backsides shifting during years of long sermons. The congregation was well-dressed and sang traditional hymns that Helen was pleased to know, including "Holy, Holy, Holy" and "Fairest Lord Jesus." Thomas had a nice voice and he was not afraid to pick out the tenor harmony on the old tunes, which were apparently familiar to him as well. Standing side by side and holding the hymnbook between them, Helen was struck with a memory of her parents on Sunday mornings long ago. They had always attended worship services together, with Helen usually sitting next to her father, and her brother Eric on the other side of their mother. Sometimes Helen would catch the sweet looks her parents would give each other during the hymn singing, and there was something in those that seemed to help them gloss over the differences that emerged all the rest of the week. Those were some of the times Helen felt most like a family. She snuck a peek out of her left eye at Thomas, standing tall next to her, his face earnest and his brow furrowed as he sang the closing bars of "Psalm 100."

Then the sermon began and even though the pastor was fairly young, decent looking, and had a nice voice, Helen's mind soon drifted off to the observation of the hats in the pews ahead of her. Two rows in front was one made of folds of wide black ribbon that sat close around the front of the wearer's head, but more loosely in the back. On the young woman a little farther ahead and to the right was a hat made to look like a covering of pink apple blossoms. It was sweet, but it wouldn't suit her own tastes, Helen decided. Then one in the row beyond caught her eye. It was white and sewn to look like one swooping rose blossom that fit smoothly to the side of the head. Helen had just begun to covet it when her attention was seized by the rising voice of the preacher.

"Are you trying to save your life or give it away? In this great city, one can aspire to so much, but remember the words of the Lord Jesus, *He that findeth his life shall lose it: and he that loseth his life for my sake shall find it.* I ask you again, are you trying to save your life or to lose it for his sake?"

What on earth is that supposed to mean? wondered Helen.

Chapter 31

March swooped in, blustery and fierce. The wind whipped up the long straight avenues like the Amtrak Express, delivering the grime of Downtown to meet the grit of Midtown. When Helen crossed the intersections on her way to work, she squeezed her eyes and mouth shut against the windy onslaught, and the commuters barely opened their mouths to excuse themselves when they blindly stumbled into each other.

With the wind came a package for Helen via certified mail. Heinrich had finally returned the divorce papers Helen had sent months before. It took Helen all evening to get up the nerve to sign them, but she did, and just as quickly stuffed them back into the return envelope. Now it was officially over. She was free. It felt so strange. But it was what she had wanted, wasn't it?

As if the weather sensed the shift in her feelings, suddenly the driving wind gave way to sodden drizzle. Everything turned to grey, and everything dripped all the time. One Saturday morning the gray was so dreary that once coffee and breakfast were finished and the dishes done, Helen had no inspiration for the day.

"Why don't you come down to Aunt Martha's with me?" asked Rose. "She's a hoot; you'll like her."

She bent her head down and peered ominously at Helen over her glasses. "She has *summoned* me to grill me about Fred." Fred was Rose's boyfriend, if he could still be called that. Rose had met him through mutual theater friends at the end of the year and had been quite serious about him from the start. He was a writer—or at least he hoped to be—but until he made his fortune in storytelling, he had a day job editing in one of New York City's big publishing houses.

He'd written a musical called *Chaff in the Wind* about his Norwegian immigrant grandparents and their family in Minnesota; he told Helen the entire plot one evening when he'd come to dinner in late January. At the time Helen thought it a dull story, but the idea of a musical was interesting, and so she held her tongue and passed the salad. He was a funny looking fellow, Helen thought, for Rose to be gazing so glowingly at him. Though in his late twenties, his dark hair was graying prematurely, as well as starting to thin on top. He had a nice nose, but he wasn't very tall. Nevertheless, Rose thought him marvelous, and since she was only 5'2" herself, his height didn't seem to worry her. Mrs. Whitaker would prefer a banker or a lawyer, she knew, but a publisher was respectable enough, and Rose told Helen that she thought her father would like the idea of a writer in the family.

"If I can get Aunt Martha on his side, then she can reassure Mother and Daddy, and they'll listen to her."

"Then shouldn't Fred be going to meet Aunt Martha instead of me?"

"He's got to work all weekend. Besides, it'll be better if I can set the stage a bit, if you know what I mean."

"I don't."

"Well, you will soon enough."

Aunt Martha lived down in Greenwich Village. It seemed an out of place locale for a wealthy maiden aunt, but Aunt Martha was not ordinary in any sense.

"Well, well!" she cried as she flung open the door to her small second floor apartment. "How in blazes are you?" As she reached across the threshold to embrace her aunt, Rose shot Helen a smirk and a raised eyebrow. Aunt Martha towered over her diminutive niece, had large feet and hands, and large expressions to go with them. She saw Helen and opened her eyes wide.

"So you brought your roomie along too, eh? It's about time. I'm Aunt Martha." She stuck out her hand, gave Helen a glare that the latter supposed was meant to be friendly, and gave Helen a handshake that shook her whole arm. "I have a last name, but no one ever uses it. Only get it out now for special occasions. Pleased to meet ya, come in, come in."

Aunt Martha's tall frame was clothed in the Gibson Girl styles that had been in vogue in her young maidenhood, some fifty years previously, with a high-necked white blouse and a long skirt that flowed from a waist that, if it wasn't narrow and petite now, surely had been in 1915. On her head she wore a sort of house bonnet that looked like a pink paisley doily with a laced fringe, out from under which stuck bits of untidy gray curls. When she turned and led the way into her flat, one long thick gray braid hung down her back and swung side to side in rhythm with her sturdy gait.

"I've got a surprise for you girls! Annie's here. Was comin' over for the poker game later on, but then decided to come early to visit a bit and see you girls."

"You ever told your roomie about her, Rosie?" They were at the end of the short hallway now and at the doorway to the sitting room. Turning into the room and without waiting for an answer, Aunt Martha said, "She's a *nun*!" She said it the way Edgar McCarthy might have denounced someone as a communist on the House floor. "So she's *Sister* to you."

"Oh, be quiet, Martha!" came a small voice from a large red armchair in the cluttered room. The voice belonged to a small old woman with a wrinkled, smiling face and dark shining eyes. She swung her hand at Aunt Martha as if to swoosh away a fly. "Rose dear, your aunt is as troublesome as always! But aren't you a sweet vision?!"

Aside from her one snap at Aunt Martha, the Sister was just the picture of what Helen might have conjured up for a nun. She was dressed in a plain long black skirt and blouse, but her hair was pulled back in a wimple and she wore a small wooden cross on a silver chain around her neck. Her smile was serene and her eyes twinkly. She kept smiling and patting Rose, who seemed delighted to see the old woman. Rose moved a pile of books that lay on the blue couch and sat on the end nearest to the old woman while they kept chattering.

"We were at school together back when we were just bitty little things. She was called *Anne* then," Aunt Martha explained to Helen as she clumped heavily about, moving another pile from off of the couch onto the floor. She waved vaguely, indicating, Helen assumed, that she should sit down. She did.

"Buuuut," she straightened up, "then we grew up. She went and got her heart broke, and I ended up with a dead soldier for a fiancé. After we'd cried on each other's shoulders for a bit, she went to join the convent, just like in the Middle Ages, and changed her name! To *Felicity* of all things! Crazy Catholics." She said the last words pointedly at her friend, who stopped just long enough in her conversation to glare sweetly at her friend.

"Never went in for all that mumbo-jumbo; everyone knows God's a sensible Presbyterian, but other than that, we've stuck together all these years. No fun being irritating all on your own!"

"No! So now we irritate each other, quite happily!" said Sister Felicity. Then she looked at Helen. "I'm afraid I've been very rude, I was just so excited to see Baby Rose here. It's been years!"

Helen, who since walking through the door had hardly had a chance to say a word, now found her voice. "Baby Rose??"

"Oh... yes, I'm Baby Rose!" Rose laughed.

"I don't suppose I should call you that anymore now, should I?" said the little nun.

"Oh, it's alright, I don't mind if it's you. Aunt Martha's out of the question, though," she tossed in the direction of her great Aunt. Aunt Martha looked at Helen and shook her head sadly, as if in sorrow at modern youth and their uppity ways.

It was charming to see Rose in such an atmosphere of longtime affection. She was obviously well-loved by both these old ladies and her personality blossomed in a way Helen had never seen it elsewhere. The seriousness that seemed to make up so much of who Rose was had fallen away, and between the two women she seemed like a small sweet girl with two doting aunties. She turned to Helen.

"Only Sister Felicity can call me Baby Rose, so don't get any ideas!" Then a more thoughtful expression came over her round face. She took the nun's wrinkled hand in her smooth white one and patted it. "I've always thought of her as my guardian angel. She brought me to my parents." She looked at the old woman fondly. "I've never told you this, Helen, but I was adopted as a baby. I'll always be grateful to Sister Felicity for bringing me to such a loving family."

"Which I am part of, let me remind you," put in Aunt Martha. "It wouldn't have happened if I hadn't been around, too. Just because she's a *nun* doesn't mean she can get all the credit." She winked at Helen.

"Oh, I know, Auntie, but Sister Felicity gets credit precisely because she doesn't demand it. And you know it."

"Oh, girls!" said the nun, shaking her head, "bicker, bicker, bicker! You are obviously in the family God intended; you are exactly like your Aunt!"

That stopped Rose in her tracks and she looked at Helen in mock surprise. Helen wasn't sure Rose wanted to be considered exactly like Aunt Martha.

"Anyway, that's why I still get to call her Baby Rose. And nobody else does," Sister Felicity added with a smug glance at her friend. For a tiny old nun, Helen thought she had an awful lot of spunk. "She came to us when the roses started to bloom. That's how she got her name."

"It's a lovely story," said Helen.

But there was something about it. Something familiar. Aunt Martha was bringing out the tea and cake now, and Helen was ready for a snack. But the something grew in her mind and wouldn't let her ignore it. It made her think. *When the roses began to bloom.* That was it. She had heard somebody else say that very same thing not too long ago. It sounded so poetic. It wouldn't have been Thomas. Or her mother. Who had said it? Maybe she'd read it in a book.

"Cream and sugar, please," she said as Aunt Martha offered. But now her mind was turning the phrase over and over. She was sure that she had heard someone say it out loud. And then she heard it in her mind's ear with a slight accent. Clementine.

With a thud it came to her. Clementine had said that about her own baby. The baby girl she'd given up. The one she'd given birth to when she stayed at the Catholic convent with the Sister who had been so kind to her. The hair on the back of Helen's neck stood up. She took a sip of her tea and tried not to spill it. Aunt Martha was cutting the cake clumsily and sending showers of crumbs down onto the carpeted floor.

What if Rose was Clementine's baby? It was a ridiculous thought and she quickly dismissed it. Just as quickly, the thought sprang up again, like a buttercup. What if she really was?

What am I thinking, thought Helen? *Thomas is right, I am not serious enough. It's a preposterous scenario.* All the same, she remembered the last preposterous scenario in her life. She had ridiculed Thomas' ideas about Vladimir, but he had been proven right. Sometimes life really was stranger than fiction.

Helen stole a peek at Rose sitting at the far end of the couch and listening to Sister Felicity. The profile. Small straight nose, rounded chin, dark curly hair and eyebrows. The profile was the same.

Oh God, help me please.

Why hadn't she ever seen it before? How could she have? Why would she have? It was too ludicrous, too much like a Shakespearean drama. The city was so big and her part of it was so small. She hadn't even known Rose was adopted until just this minute.

She looked over at Rose again, who this time turned to Helen. The eyes were completely different, but the face was so similar to Clementine's that Helen felt ridiculous for not seeing it before.

"Do you feel alright, Helen? You look kind of pale all of a sudden."

"I'm fine!" squeaked Helen, then coughed. "The cake is delicious!" she added and then hurriedly took her first bite of it.

Clementine had told her the nun's name, what had it been? She couldn't remember. She vaguely heard Rose telling the older ladies about Fred while her mind went slowly over the details again.

Then she interrupted, "Excuse me, which order did you say you belonged to, Sister?"

Felicity looked up at her blankly, then blinked her dark eyes.

"I am a Sister of Divine Providence, dear. We work among the immigrants coming to New York. I should probably say *worked*, as I don't do as much now as I'd like because of my health. But then there are not as many arriving now as there used to be in the 20s and 30s. We have a residence over on East 23rd for some of the young women just getting to America. It's a safe place to stay and then we try to help them find reputable work until they can learn English and make their way on their own."

Helen took in this information and mulled it over while sipping another cup of tea. For the rest of the hour the ladies chatted, and when Helen explained her work at The Committee to the two older ladies, she had the satisfaction of their being appropriately impressed. But all the while she kept stealing glances at Rose, wondering if and how her suspicions could be true.

Chapter 32

"You will simply not believe what I have to tell you!" Helen told Thomas the next day.

They had met again for church on East 91st and were now strolling down the eastern side of the Central Park Reservoir. The rain of the previous day had exhausted itself, and the sky was filled with white puffy clouds with patches of blue between. The cherry trees under which they walked mimicked the scene in the sky, each one a fluffy pink cloud of blossoms, and every small gust of breeze sent out a shower of pale petals, swirling around joyfully on the breeze before falling to land on the water.

"But if I won't believe it, then why will you bother to tell me?" asked Thomas in a voice that was almost petulant. In the service this morning he had seemed more distracted than usual. Helen couldn't decide if he looked more angry or dejected. Now as they walked, he looked down at her small white-gloved hand swinging by her side, and then shoved both of his further in his pockets.

"Oh, Thomas, don't be so annoying! Be a good dear friend as always, won't you?" She half turned her head and looked up at him from the corners of her eyes, smiling coyly. For an instant, Thomas looked like he might really get angry. Then he seemed to make some agreement with himself, released a sigh, and gazed back down at her with a look that spoke of devotion. Helen was pleased.

"Alright, go on, tell me the big news that got you out of bed and to church this morning."

So Helen proceeded to recount yesterday's visit with Aunt Martha and Sister Felicity and what she had learned there. She had to backtrack and tell him Clementine's story too, though as she did so, she confessed that perhaps she was breaking confidence and that he must swear never to tell a soul. He stopped abruptly on the path and faced her. A young girl on a bicycle swerved quickly to avoid him.

"Helen, I'm not one of your little school friends! If she shared something in confidence, you should not have told me. I don't care if I've never met her or if I never will. It's *her* life and *her* story."

"But don't you see? I just had to talk to someone!" Helen walked to a green park bench just off the path and set herself primly on it. Thomas sat down on the other end and turned to face her.

"I was about to burst with such a secret, and the two people I usually talk over things with are the two people about which I had to talk! I know it sounds ridiculous, like something out of a Shakespeare play, but Thomas, I have such a feeling in my inner being."

Thomas sighed heavily and shook his head. "What evidence do you have besides the feeling in your 'inner being' and the fact that there's a nun involved. Do you know how many nuns there are in New York City?"

"Well, I checked Rose's birthdate last night on her driver's license, when she wasn't looking, after I called you. I knew it was sometime in the early summer, but it's the tenth of June! And I'm almost sure that's the same date Clementine told me! I just have to make sure and then I can tell them both. Who do you think I should tell first?"

For a moment, the look of incredulity that washed over Thomas' face gave her pause.

"Are you out of your mind, Helen? You can't just barge into someone's life and tell them the deepest secrets about who they are!"

"I'm *not* barging into their lives! They are already both in my life. That's the point. I think it's my duty to tell them the truth." She pronounced the word 'duty' with a tone filled with her newly found sense of altruism.

"Well, I think it's your *duty* to keep your mouth shut. Have you thought about the possibility that neither of them wants to know all that information? There's a reason Clementine gave up her baby and didn't tell anyone, and that reason probably still exists."

"But Thomas, she *had* to give up her baby. She didn't want to, not really. She knew it was the best thing for her daughter at the time, but she's been so sad all these years, wondering what happened to her. And then just think that I'll get to tell her that's she's really very well, and very nearby."

Helen replayed the scene where she would gently tell Clementine what had happened to her long lost daughter. She had already imagined it all last night. Clementine would weep softly on her shoulder, then break down utterly. Helen would wrap her arm around her friend and nod comfortingly. Then Rose would come in and fall down at her mother's feet, and the two would embrace while Helen looked on benevolently as a high priestess of mended relationships. Then they would turn and thank her endlessly for reuniting them, acknowledging that she had made it all possible. It was a beautiful picture.

"Has it even occurred to you that Rose may not want to know anything about it? She seems very happy as she is and she has wonderful parents. Why would you want to upset her—upset all of them—all of a sudden?"

Helen was annoyed and frustrated to be yanked out of her lovely reverie.

"Oh, Thomas! Do you think I don't think at all? Do you think I'm a complete idiot?!"

Two older gentleman wearing dark suits were walking by and looked their direction, startled at the rising tone of her voice. Then they both glanced at Thomas, as if to make sure he wasn't threatening his companion. Thomas glared sullenly back at them and then leaned back on the bench, his arms folded across his chest.

"No, Helen. But sometimes I do think you are rather sel--" He stopped himself. Then he began again more slowly. "I think that you are someone who acts without always considering things from the perspective of others."

"That is absolutely ridiculous! I've done nothing but think of them from the beginning! Why on earth else would God bring me into both their lives and give me all the pieces of information? What else am I supposed to do with it?"

Here Thomas was stumped. He stretched out his long legs and looked out across the water. Then he rubbed his face with his hands. He had such nice hands, Helen thought inconveniently at that moment. Strong without roughness, gentle without languidity. She wondered for an instant what it would be like to hold one of those hands. She never had, not really.

Thomas sat up again. He reached out toward Helen and cupped her cheek in one of those nice hands. She was taken aback. Then he spoke slowly and deliberately.

"Helen, you are the most wonderful and the most frustrating woman I have ever known. Maybe you're right and you are supposed to tell them. Just please, take your time and think it through."

He paused, looking at her, his laughing green eyes quiet, his hand still touching her face. His hand was so warm there; it calmed her. She didn't want it to move. That fact surprised her, and she was confused. Helen felt her cheeks turning pink. Once upon a time, with Heinrich, with Vladimir, she would have been pleased, knowing that a blush made her face prettier and helped bring the gentleman around to her own point of view. But now with Thomas it just made her frustrated. More than ever she wanted him to take her seriously.

And at the same time, she was annoyed with him. He had been starting to say she was selfish, then, just before. She was sure that was what he'd been going to say. How could he think that? She didn't want him to think that! She wanted him to take his hand away, and yet she wished he wouldn't. Her lips parted to speak, but despite all the thoughts tumbling around in her mind, she couldn't grab on to one single thing to say. Instead, she saw Thomas' eyes looking into hers, growing clearer, getting nearer, seeing her for what she really was.

Despite the freshness of the March day, the air between them on the bench was charged and still, like the moment just before a thunderstorm. Thomas' tall lean body was moving closer to hers, bending down. His lips just brushed hers as she jumped to her feet and out of reach. She was angry with him, after all. He had called her selfish, or at least been about to.

They looked at each other again, now from about four feet away.

"Thomas!"

"Helen, I'm sorry, I just... Well, no, I'm not sorry."

"What on earth do you mean?"

"Listen, there's something else I need to tell you that has nothing to do with Clementine or Rose or anybody." He slid himself back to the far end of the bench and waved at the space next to him.

"I won't try anything, don't worry. But I'm not sorry for wanting to kiss you." Helen eyed the seat suspiciously and then sat down gingerly. "I've decided something I've been thinking about for awhile. I'm changing my plans. I don't want to wait years and years to teach, and then teach to a bunch of bored graduate students. It's the stuff I'm studying that makes me want to teach when it makes a difference. Young kids, junior high kids. And I want to start now. I've applied a few places, but I'll probably end up leaving New York." They sat for a minute in silence.

"Where will you go?" asked Helen uncertainly. She had already had a weekend's worth of revelations, and this new one of Thomas'—while not earth shattering, and while she had no claim on him but friendship, and now perhaps on some of his feelings—left her feeling suddenly insecure, like someone was tearing up her roots.

"I'm hoping to go north. I've got an aunt in Massachusetts who knows someone in administration at Deerfield Academy. It's a long shot, but I'd love to teach there."

"Oh," said Helen, who couldn't think of anything better to say. Her loss for words was unfamiliar and disconcerting.

"So I'll probably be leaving in June, when classes here are finished."

He stared at a spot on the grass nearby.

"I just thought you'd like to know."

Chapter 33

April, April
Laugh thy golden laughter
Then the moment after
Weep thy silver tears.

"That's pretty," said Helen as she looked out the rain streaked window that she was wiping dry on the inside. "Did you write it?"

"Oh, no, it's one I had the girls in my class memorize. It seemed rather appropriate for today," she added dryly as she gazed out the kitchen window to the sky which had been bright and sunny not twenty minutes before.

Rose and Helen were spring cleaning. Inspired by the fresh air and bright sunshine with which the day had dawned, they had seized the moment and pulled buckets, rags, and the broom and mop out of the closet and set to work. A week had quickly passed since their visit to Aunt Martha's. Despite her anger at Thomas, Helen had nevertheless heeded his advice and kept quiet, waiting for the right moment to sound out Rose. As they both worked quietly, Helen on the windows and Rose sorting out the kitchen cupboards, it occurred to Helen that this might be as good a moment as she could get. She finished the window pane where she was working and moved on into the kitchen. Rose stood on a chair, emptying the top cupboard onto the counter. Packages of rice and noodles and cans of tuna lined up neatly in front of her, awaiting orders.

Helen tried to choose a casual tone.

"Rose, I've been thinking about what you said last week."

"Hmmm?" answered Rose, absentmindedly, from her perch.

"I mean about Sister Felicity and being adopted and all. Have you ever wondered who your mother might be? Your real mother?"

Rose took her head out of the cupboard she was wiping and dropped her rag in a bucket of ammonia water. It made a squelchy sound, and a wave of acrid odor dispersed into the air.

"Alice Whitaker is my real mother. You mean my biological mother."

"Well, yes, I mean your biological mother then. Do you know anything about her? Don't you ever wonder what happened to her?"

"No. No, I don't." There was an edge to Rose's voice. She squeezed out her rag noisily and went back to cleaning.

"Really? Not ever? Surely sometimes you must wonder a little bit."

"No, Helen." There was that shortness again. She took her head out of the cupboard and glanced out the window across the room. The sun was once more peeking through the clouds. She blinked, set her jaw and looked straight at her roommate.

"My mother is the woman who raised me, who made my breakfast each morning, who helped me with my homework, who sat with me in the steamy bathroom at night when the croup was so bad I could barely breathe. I'm a practical person. The woman who gave birth to me wanted to be free of me and she gave me away. If she didn't want me, then I don't have the time to spare a thought for her."

It sounded so harsh.

"But what if she felt she didn't have a choice? What if she believed it was for your good?"

"Well fine, then. But it doesn't change who my mother is. Or who she will be."

"What if it was really hard? What if it was the hardest thing she'd ever done?"

Rose looked her strangely, trying to understand what had come over her roommate.

"What do you mean, Helen?"

"Well, I'm not so sure I understand this self-sacrifice thing myself. I'm just learning. But what if her decision wasn't made so that she could be free, but so you could be? And what if that cost her all the things that mattered?" The words felt odd on her tongue.

Rose didn't say anything. She stood perched on her chair, not even moving. The wind outside blew in gusts against the pane. The sun was shining freely now, but in the distance darker clouds threatened another shower.

"It doesn't change anything. I suppose it might make me think better of her, but my life is here and now, with my real mother and father. Like I said, I'm a practical person."

And with that Rose turned back to cleaning. The conversation seemed to have ended, so Helen picked up her rag and did the same.

Chapter 34

The Russian Tea Room was ablaze with light and color. Helen sat across from Ivan at one of the booths along the wall toward the back of the restaurant. The red leather seat felt luxurious against her back and the wait staff was very attentive. The golden sculpted firebirds on the wall caught and reflected the lamplight. She smiled across the table at Ivan. He finished ordering their drinks in Russian and smiled back at her.

"It's very good of you to join me this evening," said Ivan.

"Well, thank you for the invitation. The show was a smash, don't you think?"

Ivan furrowed his brows, turning them into a single dark brush stroke over his face.

"I don't know. *New Girl in Town* is so American. You Americans must always have a happy ending, no matter how unlikely. Look at how they changed the sad ending in *Pygmalion* to a happy one in *My Fair Lady*. There must always be a happy ending." Then he raised his eyebrows high. They broke into two pieces, "But maybe that is why everyone likes America!" and Ivan looked extra surprised. Helen smiled in spite of herself. A fellow couldn't help his God-given eyebrows after all. He wasn't so bad. In fact she had decided in the last few days that he was rather nice. When he'd stopped by her desk Thursday afternoon to ask her out, she was glad her Saturday was free. It was a nice distraction from thinking about Rose and Clementine. She couldn't admit it, but it was also a nice distraction from thinking about Thomas. She had never thought of Thomas as more than a far-off admirer—he was not a suitor she could ever take seriously—but she couldn't stop remembering how nice his hand had felt against her cheek that Sunday a few weeks ago and how conflicted she felt at the news that he was leaving.

"Have you heard anything more of Vladimir?" asked Ivan quietly.

Helen, jolted back to the present, shook her head. After the news a couple months ago that he'd been transferred in custody to a secure location outside of Washington, DC, there had been no more news, and no one in the office wished to appear eager to find out any. Ivan shook his dark heavy head as well.

"The whole business is a pity for the Committee, but you know, Helen, as it pertains to you, I am glad that he is no longer here." Across the table he gave Helen a long gaze from under his brows, his dark eyes impenetrable. She assumed it was a look meant to convey attachment and affection. All Helen felt was awkward. She liked the attention and the fine surroundings of the theatre and the restaurant. And she'd liked the thought of a date with Ivan and his eyebrows. She felt ashamed that she had ever laughed at him with Pansy, like a couple of stupid school girls. Ivan was a good person. Without the least attempt to play with her feelings, he had invited her out to a Broadway show and now out to an expensive restaurant. The mere thought of such circumstances would have thrilled Helen a few months ago, but somehow, being out on the town didn't fill her with excitement in the same way, and she wasn't sure why.

Their cocktails arrived, two swirling glasses of potent liquid that looked almost green. Helen took a sip, and the alcohol burned its way down her throat. Her eyes stung. Ivan watched her worriedly.

"I am sorry," he said. "It may be that it is a little strong. We can order you something else."

"Mmmm...well, oh it's alright. Oh...well maybe. But what on earth is it called?"

Ivan looked sheepish. "It's one of their special drinks here. It's not even very Russian, no vodka—a mixture of whisky and rum and something else, but..." He smiled the smile of a shy little boy and looked into his glass. "I couldn't resist. They call it 'Ivan the Terrible.'"

Chapter 35

Rose was now officially engaged. Fred had taken her on a day outing and proposed on the Staten Island Ferry. Helen couldn't help thinking it was a fairly prosaic setting for a proposal, what with the orange paint and all, but Rose didn't seem to mind a bit, nor the fact that they hadn't even been on the view side of the ship at the time.

Aunt Martha was true to her word, and with her commendation, Fred was now welcomed into the family by the Whitakers. Rose was exceedingly happy, and that made Helen happy too. She was a little wistful, thinking back on her own engagement. But as Rose liked to say of herself, she was a practical person and she had a very practical engagement, nothing like the whirlwind chaos that Helen's own had been.

As if foreseeing that their daughter would refuse too much extravagance at her wedding, Mr. and Mrs. Whitaker countered with a plan to spread the festivities out. Rose could plan the wedding, but they would throw her an engagement party on their own terms at the end of the summer at High Hills, their country club. And for such an occasion, Rose needed a dress. Much as she hated to admit it, nothing she already owned would quite fit the occasion.

"What was the name of that seamstress Aunt Martha told you about back in the fall?" Rose asked Helen one evening. "Mother is insisting on paying for a new dress." It was mid-May, and such a balmy warm breeze floated on the air that all the windows in the apartment, as well as the doors to the terrace, were wide open. They were sitting out on the terrace with glasses of wine enjoying the long late twilight. Helen loved twilight. It always made her feel thoughtful, rather wistful and hopeful at the same time. But now Rose's question jolted her away from her thoughts.

"Oh. The seamstress? Uh...Clementine. Her name is Clementine Cavaziel." It had been days since she had thought about Clementine and Rose, and she was almost ready to believe that she'd imagined the whole secret relationship.

"She's not far away, is she?"

"No, she's not. Just down on 82nd."

"Well," said Rose, getting up, "do you still have her number? Maybe I'll just give her a call right now, and go over next week before school is out. Otherwise I'll just put off the whole thing until it's too late."

Helen fished out the number, and then gave it uneasily to Rose. Fortunately, Rose was too purposeful to notice anything wrong on Helen's face. Helen perched carefully on the couch and picked up a magazine to thumb through nonchalantly while she listened to Rose's end of the conversation. It was very matter of fact. Helen felt silly. Had she been expecting their voices to give the secret away?

"Very good, that's settled," said Rose as she hung up the phone. "Next Thursday evening."

"Can I go with you?" asked Helen, perhaps a little too eagerly.

Rose peered at her. "Sure. I mean, if you really want to. It won't be very exciting."

Helen was worried for a second that Rose suspected something, but actually she seemed pleased.

"Oh, I think it will be fun! And besides, Clementine's a dear, and it's been awhile since I've seen her."

So the following Thursday, the young women met when Helen left work and made their way over to 82nd Street. Waiting outside Clementine's door, Helen was half expecting to feel some electric charge in the air when the door opened and Clementine saw her daughter. But instead, Clementine saw Helen first and smiled warmly as she greeted both women. She led them down the hall into the sitting room that was now familiar to Helen. The air was scented with ginger.

"I've just made some spice bread. Would you girls like some?"

In the sitting room, Helen waited for something to happen, but things progressed as one might expect. After pleasantries were exchanged over slices of spice bread, along with greetings from Aunt Martha, they briefly discussed what kind of dress to make and then Clementine started taking Rose's measurements. Helen sat in the green armchair, not saying anything for once, watching the two women. Now that she saw them side by side, she saw that there were plenty of physical differences of course, but the similarities were striking. She wondered that neither of them seemed to notice.

"When will the wedding be?" asked Clementine after a little while.

"Not until next June, I'm afraid, because Fred wants to wait until he knows whether or not his musical will fly. That's why Mother insisted on a party sooner."

"Ah, well June is a lovely month for a wedding."

"Yes, but late June, well after the 10th. I don't want to share my wedding anniversary and my birthday."

Helen looked up then. Rose was standing straight in her stocking feet with her eyes on the painting of the Alps, while Clementine knelt beside her, measuring tape in hand.

"Oh. Your birthday is June 10th." Clementine said this matter of factly, nodding to herself. Her back straightened and she leaned back on her heels, looking sharply at Rose.

Then she changed the subject.

"So you girls are the same age?"

"Oh, no, I'm the older one," said Rose. She smiled mischievously at Helen. "Helen's just a baby; she was born in '31 and I was born in '30. That's why I get to boss her around."

"Ah." Clementine said simply. Then she rose to her feet and gave Rose another intent look. "Excuse me a moment, please," and she abruptly left the room.

Rose sat back down and the young women looked at each other. Rose raised her eyebrows in question, and Helen shrugged. Rose picked up the copy of *Time* magazine that lay on the coffee table. On the cover was a photo of Jordan's dashing young King Hussein, wearing his military uniform and his black and white headscarf, giving a speech to his followers. Helen sat uneasily for a moment, and then got up.

"I guess I'll just go check if she needs help with something."

Helen found Clementine in the kitchen, huddled with her back to the counter and chewing on her knuckles. She looked up at Helen with a questioning expression.

"I'm so sorry," she began. "I was just distracted by something. But it's nothing, really..." her voice trailed off. She opened her mouth to speak again, but nothing came out.

Helen took a deep breath.

"Rose was adopted," she exhaled quickly and quietly, afraid of what her news might do to the older woman. "She was born on June 10th and adopted with the help of a nun called Sister Felicity."

The look on Clementine's face changed from one of question to disbelief.

"It cannot be true! I thought I was dreaming it up, but you say it's true!" she said incredulously.

"I know it seems impossible. Or at least highly unlikely. But it seems to be true." Helen didn't know what else to say.

Clementine's look transformed from disbelief to hope and then to anger. "Why did you bring her here?" she hissed.

"She wanted to come. For her dress! She would have come anyway, without me. And...I wasn't sure. Now I think I am."

"I...I... I don't know what to say. I don't know what to think!" Clementine wrung her hands and looked around the kitchen frantically, as if she would find the reasons there why her long-lost daughter had just appeared in her sitting room.

Helen had never seen her anything near like this, so lost, so out of control. She couldn't think of anything to say herself.

Finally, Clementine's self-control returned. She passed her hand over her eyes and then smoothed her skirt.

"You had better go."

They went back across the hall together, Helen in the lead. Rose looked up as they entered. Clementine, half hidden behind Helen, spoke in a voice that was surprising in its firmness.

"I'm afraid I'm not feeling very well. But I've got the measurements I need, and I'll begin the work."

She chanced a quick look at Rose. Then she added in a shakier voice, "I'm terribly sorry."

"Oh, it's not a problem. I guess you've got what you need then." Rose seemed perplexed but was not really concerned. "I do hope you feel better straightaway," she said as she gathered up her things.

"Yes, yes, I'm sure I will. I'll just lay down for a bit," said Clementine as she showed them to the door. Rose walked out first and started down the stairs. Helen stood a minute, fumbling with her jacket. Clementine took advantage of the moment to lean forward and whisper, her face pale, her eyes drawn, "She's a good person, isn't she? She's done very well?"

Helen looked back into her dark, worried eyes and nodded silently.

Chapter 36

It was a gorgeous June day. Even a day at the office did not dampen anyone's spirits, and for that matter, everyone there seemed inclined to cut the day short and get outside into the gentle sunshine and fresh air. At 5:05 Helen stepped outside onto the street. Though generally allergic to exercise, she had resolved to walk up through Central Park and clear her thoughts in the greenness for a while.

"I'll come with you," said Pansy when she heard Helen's plan. Helen didn't really feel conversational, but Pansy's comfortable chatter was pleasant enough company until she turned off to do some errand on 57th Avenue.

Helen continued the last two blocks, past the glitzy shops that faced 5th Avenue, but their storefronts and glamorous contents had lost their appeal for her today. She crossed in front of the Plaza Hotel, barely giving it a glance, and crossed into the park. With a sense of relief she entered the leafy coolness and left the hard shapes of the city temporarily behind her.

She walked slowly, making her way up the east side of the park, but even so, by the time she reached the Conservatory Water her feet were complaining about walking in heels. She found a bench near the boat house and sat to watch the children launch model sailboats onto the water. There was not much wind and the boats drifted near the shore. The water was perfectly smooth. A few puffy, white clouds drifted gently across the sky to the west, but for the most part the sky was an empty deep blue and the still water reflected it perfectly. Helen sighed. It was so calm. It made her feel calm, too, and she needed that. She wanted to feel like that lovely still water, that empty blue.

She stood up and stepped forward, sitting on the stone rim that formed the lake's edge, peering down at her own reflection. Her brown hair curled softly around her shoulders, and her blue eyes sparkled. She smiled at herself, a well-practiced demure smile. Her red lipsticked lips pulled up on one corner of her mouth as she gazed sidelong at herself in the water. All of a sudden she had to laugh at herself. It felt good to laugh. There were so many weighty things to consider.

Thomas was leaving and in the busyness of his preparations she hadn't had a chance to talk to him about what had happened at Clementine's apartment. She felt so ambiguous about him. He seemed to be the one man who could see through the well-practiced smiles that floated on her surface like the reflection of her face on the lake. He knew where and what she was coming from and all about Heinrich. But he still cared for her and wanted her. He had told her as much again the last time they spoke a few days before. She had never wanted to take him seriously, but he was making that difficult. He had given her an ultimatum.

"Helen, I love you," he had said. He had spoken plainly, not without emotion, but in spite of it. They had gone out for the day to the Jersey Shore for a pleasant, casual Saturday on the sand. It had been such a nice uncomplicated day, windblown and refreshing. They laughed together watching the other couples and families with young toddlers shrieking in the waves. All Helen's makeup wore off, and she didn't care. Thomas didn't seem to notice, but kept smiling at her with his merry eyes. They had brought a picnic lunch of egg salad sandwiches and root beer, and after lunch Thomas went for ice cream cones and came back licking the sides of both of them—mint for her, chocolate for him—to tidy up the melting drips. It was one of those days that made Helen wish they could all be like that. As dusk fell they came back to town for dinner in the Café Voykop just down from Helen's apartment. They had changed out of their sandy beach clothes, but Helen couldn't help thinking that Thomas seemed much less at home here than with their picnic lunch on the beach.

"I love you, and it's been a wonderful day," said Thomas suddenly, after their salads had come and gone. He had looked her straight in the eye. "It's the kind of day I would like to go on forever. But I don't know if you feel the same way, or if this is just an amusing way to spend a Saturday until someone more interesting, more cosmopolitan, comes along. And I want to know, Helen. I need to know...if you take me seriously. If you even take life seriously enough for our friendship to continue. Damn it all, I don't want just a *friend*, Helen. I think you know what I mean. And I need to know that you *do* care." He paused and rubbed his forehead with his hand. Then he ran his fingers through his hair so that it all stood up on end, like the first time she had seen him on the bus. He sat back and looking down at his hands on the table, he continued slowly.

"I think that if you're just playing with me, if you just want me around as an accessory for a while, then I'd better just move away and move on." He swallowed and raised his gaze to hers, above the flickering candle on the white tablecloth.

Helen had looked across at him, all a muddle at his declaration. "But...what do you want me to say?" He expected something big of her, she knew, but she was so uncertain. She hardly knew herself what she wanted.

"Get serious. Make up your mind what you want and go after it. Stop dilly-dallying and fluttering about in people's lives. Life isn't just going to wait around for you, you know. If what you want is me, than I am a happy, happy man. And if you don't, then the sooner I know that for sure, the better."

Helen bit her bottom lip and nodded silently, looking at Thomas across the table. His clear eyes gazed at her intently. She recalled the first time she'd met him, stepping off of the bus months ago. He'd seemed so funny and carefree, but as she reflected now on his words, his actions, it seemed to her that he was one of the most intentional men she knew.

They had finished up their meal in silence and walked up the street quietly, Thomas with his hands stuffed firmly in his pockets. Though it was past ten o'clock, there had still been light in the long June evening and dusk was settling over the city. The faint perfume of wisteria floated from somewhere. The air was an ideal temperature. Just down the block from her building, they paused. Angelo stood outside the building, but discreetly kept his attention turned the other direction.

"Do you...want to come up?" Helen had asked uncertainly.

"No. It would be better to say goodbye now. You know what I think. You need time to think, too. Take a week, a month and think, ponder, pray, postulate, reflect, resume, meditate, pray some more." His face cracked into his familiar smile as he looked down at her. In the flow of his words, his weighty seriousness that made her nervous all but vanished. But then he added, "Think, Helen, and then tell me...let me know by the beginning of August. If I don't hear anything from you, I'll know your answer."

He leaned down and kissed her. One soft, warm, enveloping kiss that lingered and seemed a distillation of the warm kindness of the summer air swirling around them. Then Thomas straightened up resolutely. He brushed her left cheek with his hand and turned to walk away.

"Then this is goodbye?" Helen asked weakly. This wasn't how she'd imagined this going at all.

He turned again to look at her, his eyes blinking, his lips pressed together.

"That part is up to you." Then he had walked up the street and was gone.

***

Remembering how his face had looked, Helen now peered down into the reflection of her own. She tried her practiced smile again. The Helen in the lake gazed back with skeptical eyes. The water was so calm. Around the Helen in the lake, every detail of the trees showed on the surface of the water. It looked so cool and inviting, and impulsively Helen slipped her shoes off and swung her tired feet over the side of the lake. The cold water felt delicious and she wriggled her toes happily for a moment. Suddenly, something brushed against her left foot, and instinctively she drew it up out of the water. Now that her feet had broken the water's surface, she could see down into its depths. There was a dark, thick sludge lying unevenly over the bottom; one of the brownish green pond weeds had grazed her foot. Disgusted, she lifted her right foot out as well. Bits of rubbish sat half-sunken in the sludge or were caught in the grass near the shore, like lice on a sickly head of hair. Candy wrappers, cigarette butts, dead leaves, and chewing gum foil floated lazily over two rusted tin cans sitting on the bottom. Out of one of the cans still oozed the rotten remains of whatever it had contained. It broke Helen's mood.

What had seemed so serene and pure on the surface held, in fact, a mire of decomposing refuse. She longed to rinse off her feet, to remove the contamination, but the only water nearby was that from which she had just taken them. There was nothing she could do. So now she sat at the lake's edge, her dripping feet making a dark puddle on the pavement, feeling ridiculous. A moment ago she'd felt carefree and impulsive and original, and now all she felt was ridiculous. Her stockings were wet and clammy on her legs, and with her pumps splayed in the puddle on the ground next to her, she made an interesting sight in the eyes of the two mothers pushing baby buggies on the path. They glanced at each other, raising their eyebrows. Helen stood and turned away from the women, brushed off her skirt, stepped angrily back into her pumps, and started off in the direction of home. What else could she do?

Chapter 37

July was hot. Stiflingly hot. Unbearably hot. For Independence Day Helen had been invited to the Whitakers', and it had been the kind of July 4th one read about in magazines. A pleasantly warm morning spent at a small-town parade full of shiny red fire trucks, and a long afternoon of grilled steak and corn on the cob at long tables covered with red-and-white-checked tablecloths set up in the grassy shade. In the evening there were fireworks over the football field at the local high school. It had been delicious to be outside as the fireflies danced above the grass, making their own miniature fireworks display. But when the weekend was over Helen returned to the city and the stones and work and her thoughts. Then the heat began to build.

Each day the thermometer crept higher in the glass on the apartment balcony, and the untiring rays of the sun began to feel like prison bars trapping Helen in their grip. At work there was air conditioning and the blessed coolness helped to temper the frustration at being stuck indoors all day long. In their apartment Helen and Rose kept fans running every moment that they were home and took showers before bed to cool off before lying down in their thin cotton nightgowns in front of the fans. By the third week of July, Rose had had enough. The summer school session over now, she retreated back to her parents' home and out of the city.

"I feel guilty leaving you here, Helen," she said as she packed up. "But it's my chance to get away and let Fred get to know my parents better. You are always welcome, you know. My parents really like you – try to come out on the weekend."

Helen promised that she would.

But once Friday came, the effort of moving and going anywhere seemed impossible. Helen sat on the terrace, trying in vain to catch any faint breeze that might waft up. The city seemed still with so many of its residents having fled and the rest not wanting to move, holding their breath and their energy to bear the heat of the afternoon.

It's so quiet and empty, thought Helen. Empty. Nearly everyone she knew was away. Rose was gone. Pansy had gone to see family in Maine. Mr. Major had left a few days ago for Martha's Vineyard. And of course, Thomas was gone too. He was probably congratulating himself that he'd gotten out of the city before the heat wave struck. He was probably congratulating himself for being away from her and her "lack of persistence," whatever that was.

To distract herself, Helen started cleaning the apartment. It seemed an unlikely thing to do on such a hot day, but a tidy and uncluttered space always helped make things seem cooler. But as she wiped down the kitchen counters, she found, unwillingly, that her thoughts kept turning to Thomas. She told herself that she was glad that he was gone, that he had been sorely mistaken about her character and her intentions. She was not who or what he wanted. She wasn't ready for exclusivity and commitment again, she told herself as she swept the floor. She was Helen Hartmann, divorcée in New York, charming, witty, and adventurous!

But this time, as she willed herself to feel like that, it felt hollow. She didn't feel witty and adventurous. She felt used up and tired. She tried thinking of Ivan and of Vladimir, of Mr. Major and even of Heinrich, but it was no use. Mr. Major, Ivan, Pansy, and Rose would come back, but the city, her life, her future felt empty with Thomas gone.

By lunchtime the floors were clean, the carpets vacuumed and the long hot afternoon stretched before her. She couldn't stay here.

Her thoughts wandered to Clementine. She was still in the city so far as she knew. It had been a long while since she had seen Clementine, not since the day she'd seen her with Rose. It seemed odd now to Helen that she'd never gone to talk to Clementine further about that revelation. Today would be a good time for a visit, and the older woman always had something philosophical to say that did Helen good. And perhaps, she thought altruistically, a visit would do a bit of good to Clementine as well. Before she could catch the thought, she found herself wondering what Thomas would think of that, her being altruistic.

It would be an effort to get to Clementine's, but not nearly the effort it would have been to get to Connecticut. She needed a reason to get out of the apartment, and surely Clementine would have some lemonade as a reward. Helen put on the lightest linen sundress she owned and ventured out.

The bus rumbled slowly down Lexington Avenue, as if it, too, was worn out by the afternoon heat. At 82nd Helen descended and began to walk the two long blocks west. She walked slowly, the heat radiating off of the pavement like off the top of the stove top the few times she'd used it. When she got to Clementine's apartment house, she stopped and gathered her strength before beginning the climb. It was only four stories without an elevator, and she was grateful it wasn't higher, but how did Clementine manage it when Helen found herself out of breath at the top? It was all those years climbing the mountain paths, Helen decided. She made her slow way up, the air in the stairwell stuffier at each step.

At the top of the stairs she stood a moment, catching her breath. Her nose tickled. In the air was a faint acrid odor. She wrinkled her nose and forced herself to breathe a small shallow breath. She knocked on Clementine's door and waited. She strained her ears for movement inside, but no one came to the door. There was no answer to her second knock. Clementine wasn't here after all; she had made the trek through the burning streets for nothing.

Back down the stairs she slowly stepped, annoyed at Clementine for not being there, and annoyed at herself for not telephoning first. Back outside on the stoop, Helen stood still a moment. Though the heat in the streets was still oppressive, the air was remarkably fresher out here. It didn't seem right; something didn't fit. She took a deep breath. She could still smell the unpleasant odor, why couldn't she place it? It was vaguely familiar. Maybe she could place it now, out here in the comparatively fresh air where she could think more clearly than up in front of Clementine's door.

Surely Clementine was there, but then why hadn't she answered the door? Maybe Helen hadn't knocked loudly enough? Maybe Clementine had seen Helen coming and purposefully chosen not to answer. After all, their last meeting with Rose had been very upsetting. Maybe Clementine didn't want to see her. The seeds planted in her fertile mind by Thomas' careful comments had softened in the rainy season of his absence and were now beginning to sprout. Perhaps not everyone was always as glad to see her as she assumed.

If Clementine didn't want to see her, then it was just as well that she had left. Helen was never one to force an issue; wasn't it much easier and wiser to pursue a course of non-confrontation? To let happen what may? But now another of Thomas' admonitions came to her. He had called her indecisive, lacking in persistence. She had been exceedingly vexed when he had said it, but in this moment, she felt it was true. She had come here to see Clementine, she was now fairly certain that Clementine was actually there, and yet now she stood on the doorstep leaving without much effort. She *would* make an effort. She'd come to see Clementine and see her she would.

Helen turned and gazed up at the windows of Clementine's apartment which looked out on 82nd, half expecting to see a woman's face at the pane. Instead, she saw tendrils of gray smoke curling out through the open screen. Smoke! That was the smell in the stairs! Why hadn't she placed it before? Something was burning in Clementine's apartment. Helen bit her lip and wondered for too long what she should do. She always wanted to be sure of what she should do before taking any action, before any sort of commitment. Then, though she still had absolutely no idea what to do, she went back inside and ran up the stairs.

Chapter 38

The top of the stairwell was now hazy and smoke was seeping from under Clementine's door. Surely she should have noticed it before. Why hadn't she? The smoke burned her throat and made her cough. Helen covered her nose and mouth with one hand, and banged on the door with the other.

"Clementine!" she screamed, her heart pounding from her run up the stairs and from the sudden fear clawing at her heart. She kept banging. She tried the door but it was locked. And padlocked she could tell, which meant for sure that Clementine was inside, locked in with the choking smoke. Helen kept yelling the woman's name and banging, with no effect. She stepped back a pace and threw her weight against it, but only succeeded in bruising her shoulder. The brown oak door didn't budge. She turned and banged on the door opposite, but there was no answer. Helen's heart kept thudding and suddenly she felt cold and sick to her stomach. A fresh wave of perspiration rolled down her back against her sundress.

She ran down a flight of stairs, the most effort she had exerted in days. The first door she could find was under the apartment opposite Clementine's. On the door was a neat handwritten label, Mrs. Sophie Leopold. The script was spidery but elegant, and Helen's panicked vision swirled about the small letters as she pounded with both fists. The door opened quickly to her frantic knocking, revealing the frightened surprised eyes of the bony older woman Helen had passed on her first visit to Clementine's. Helen stepped back as they stared at each other for a second in fright.

"Fire!" Helen breathed finally. "There's a fire upstairs! Clementine — Miss Cavaziel -- and I can't get the door opened!"

For another second they stared at each other as the fact registered in the older lady's eyes.

"Mr. Blanchet will know what to do, he's the concierge," and she stepped out of the doorway with more alacrity than Helen expected. She sped down two flights to the ground floor and knocked loudly at the door nearest the entrance.

"He's the concierge," she repeated, "he's sure to be here now. I met him coming back only an hour ago."

Another few moments and the three were speeding back up the stairs, the burly Mr. Blanchet in the lead brandishing a crowbar. Still more agonizing minutes passed until the thick oak of the door cracked and gave and the door pushed in, nearly sending Mr. Blanchet to the floor. Thick billows of smoke curled out through the open doorway. Helen's heart sank and her eyes smarted badly from the smoke and her tears. With a roiling stomach, she followed the concierge into the apartment.

They made their way through the apartment, searching each room until they arrived at the workroom and saw Clementine lying face down on the floor. The smoke was so thick they could barely see her quiet form on the ground beneath the ironing board. The top of the board was ablaze, along with the portion of the wall against which it stood. It stood a foot away from a tall bookshelf full of volumes, which were now burning fiercely, and the blaze had already moved swiftly along to the wooden cabinet of fabric that stood just beyond. Everything in the room seemed to be smoldering. The horror of seeing Clementine's prone form overwhelmed Helen's own terror. In her concern for her friend, she barely registered the fact that she was in a burning building.

Mr. Blanchet moved quickly to Clementine's side and bent to lift her head and shoulders. Helen understood and lifted Clementine's feet and together they carried her out into the stairwell and down the stairs. Helen's head pounded from the effort and the smoke; through the pounding she could faintly hear the high-pitched whine of sirens that grew steadily louder. Mrs. Leopold had telephoned the fire department.

Later, Helen remembered only handing off their burden to strong, suited arms on the way down, and then being hustled outside while other firemen rushed past them, heading upstairs. On the street and sidewalk a crowd was gathering around the fire trucks. All the residents of the building were safely out now, standing with their neighbors, gawking upwards at Clementine's smoky windows. But where was Clementine? Helen scanned the scene and then saw a stretcher being loaded into an ambulance behind the nearest fire truck. She ran over as quickly as her wobbly legs would carry her. That was a good sign wasn't it? They didn't put the dead into ambulances, did they?

"Is she alright?" she gasped to the emergency workers carefully loading the stretcher. Clementine looked so small wrapped up in white sheets. An oxygen mask was over her nose and mouth.

"No. But she's alive...for now. We need to go."

It was hope.

Chapter 39

Two hours later Helen stood in the cold linoleum hallway of Metropolitan Hospital, waiting for news of Clementine. The nurse at the station just opposite the waiting area was businesslike and brusque. She was small and wiry, with a firm brown gaze that seemed like it would always remain unruffled despite the thousands of human tragedies she must have seen played out in her emergency room. The blue plastic tag on her white dress read Esther Johnson, RN.

"Are you next of kin?" she had asked when Helen had first made inquiries. "Then I can't give you any information yet," she said when Helen had replied in the negative. "We're trying to contact her family. If you have any information about that for us, that would be helpful."

"I don't think she has any family here," said Helen doubtfully. "She immigrated here years ago and never married."

"Ah," said the nurse matter-of-factly and scribbled something on the page in front of her.

So Helen waited, first on the cold metal folding chair, then pacing the hallway a bit trying to get warm. It was amazing how cold she could feel when it was blazing outside. But she'd left home with no sweater and now she was anxious and shivering in a cold hallway. Nurse Esther appeared suddenly beside Helen with a blanket. Perhaps she was less inured to suffering than she first appeared.

"You seem like you need this. I think the doctor will be out soon."

Doctor Solomon's black shoes squeaked as he walked down the corridor, and his large round glasses made him look like an owl, but behind them he had a caring face and eyes that peered down at Helen. Helen heard him talking quietly with Nurse Esther and glancing up in her direction before walking across to the waiting area.

"You are here with Miss Cavaziel?"

"Yes, that's right."

"What is your relation to her, if I may ask? Esther says that you are not a family relation."

"No, just a friend. I was going to visit her when her apartment caught fire. How is she?"

Seeing the look of concern on Helen's face, the doctor glanced back at the nurse and then answered.

"She will make it. But she had a very close call, and her lungs have suffered a trauma from smoke inhalation. They seem to be quite weak already and this has weakened them more."

"She told me that she had a lung condition when she was a girl."

"Ah, yes. Hmm. Well, she's alright for now. We're keeping her sedated. Can you reach her family?"

Once again Helen felt her insides wrench at the word *family*. The family Clementine had was far away and her nearest living relative didn't even know that was what she was.

"I don't think she has any family. But I'll talk to her neighbors."

Dr. Solomon nodded gravely and turned to walk away.

"Wait, doctor...can I see her?"

He half turned and shook his head. "Maybe tomorrow."

Chapter 40

Tomorrow came and went, and several more days passed by. Helen visited Clementine's neighbors to update them on Clementine's condition, and spent her time after work hovering at the hospital. Why she felt so responsible she couldn't quite explain or even understand herself. But she did, and only more so when she learned that Clementine had been ironing Rose's engagement dress when she had collapsed from the overwhelming heat. With Clementine unconscious on the floor, the iron had fallen face down on the delicate tulle fabric. First it had scorched, and then smoldered into flame.

Mr. Blanchet, the concierge, was now busy at the apartment, cleaning as best he could. Helen ended up helping him sort through the things in Clementine's workroom that could be salvaged—which were few—and those that needed to be discarded. The smoke smell pervaded everything. It was difficult to believe that the work of a fire for a few minutes could do so much damage.

Helen also made a call to the Whitakers to tell the news. Rose was aghast and sent a huge bouquet of flowers with wishes for a speedy recovery. The following Tuesday evening—a little over a week since the accident—after peeking in past the door at Clementine's sedated form, Helen didn't know what to do with herself. She felt lost and helpless. She felt restless and anxious, but for what, she was uncertain. She had gotten all caught up in someone else's life and needed some perspective. Wasn't that what Thomas had called it? She needed some perspective and a quiet place that wasn't her own apartment.

She left the hospital and started walking to Redeemer Church, where she had sat with Thomas a few weeks and a million years ago. Maybe it would be open, she thought, and she would try to find words to pray for her friend. She'd never been too good at prayer, and she wasn't too sure God would want to listen to her anyway. But perhaps He would listen if she were praying for someone else's needs, not just her own.

She remembered the last time she'd attended church there with Thomas. For once she'd been concentrating on what the minister was saying—something about the mystery and foolishness of God becoming a man—and in the midst of that, Thomas had quietly reached over and taken her hand in his. She'd glanced quickly at him, but his eyes were on the preacher, and so they had stayed like that, hand in warm comfortable hand resting on the pew between them until they stood for the closing hymn.

Now she reached the door of the old stone church and hesitated. She'd seen someone slip inside as she'd rounded the corner and now she heard noises from inside. It seemed that some kind of meeting was being held. Without someone with her, she felt awkward about going in. Maybe she wouldn't. She turned to walk away and saw an elderly couple starting up the steps. The woman wore a green pillbox hat and elegant gloves, and he was dressed in a simple but tasteful dark suit. The gentleman quickly stepped around Helen and opened the door in front of her with a smile. Though the evening wasn't dark yet, an even warmer light poured out of the church and made a bright pool in which Helen found herself standing.

"I recognize you, dear," said the woman in the green hat. "You've come a few times Sunday morning, haven't you? And tonight you've come for the foot washing service?"

"Yes," said Helen to her own surprise. "Yes, I suppose I have."

Chapter 41

Wednesday when Helen went to the hospital, Clementine was awake. She looked pale and tired. Her eyes held their usual intelligence, but looked worried and frightened above the oxygen mask that still covered her nose. Her breathing was slow and rattled.

"Helen!" she exhaled hoarsely. Her voice was very faint. She took a long slow breath. "What happened?" she took another breath. "They said you..." – *breath* – "...could tell me" - *breath*.

As relieved as Helen was at seeing her friend awake, it was awful to see her in such pain, gasping for each breath, laboring over every word. Helen sat on the chair next to the bed and slowly recounted the story of that Saturday. She explained about Rose's dress and the heat and her visit. In the telling she tried to recollect why on earth she had gone to visit Clementine in the first place. Ah yes, just to talk, to talk about Thomas. He seemed so far away now, and since Clementine wasn't fit to talk about that, she skipped over mentioning him. On Clementine's face, shame was now taking the place of fear.

"...Rose's dress... it's ruined."

"It's all right, Clementine, don't worry about that at all. Besides, Rose already knows all about it and she cares more about you than about a dress." Clementine caught her gaze and held it a long moment, as if in question.

"She sent you these," said Helen and pointed to a bright bouquet across the room. "But the doctor says you shouldn't have any flowers in your room because of the pollen. The air you breathe should be pure...but don't worry, zinnias keep forever. I'll take care of them for you until you're ready to go home."

Clementine looked sad and disappointed at the doctor's ban on flowers, but too weary for the effort to express her feelings. She sank her curly dark head back onto the white pillow and turned to Helen with a look of gratitude.

Cautiously, awkwardly, Helen picked up the pale, cool hand that lay on top of the white sheet and held it in her own. She'd never thought of her own hands as large before, but she nearly engulfed Clementine's hand between two of hers. Clementine closed her eyes and dozed, her rasping breath making the only noise in the room.

Helen sat still a long time, holding Clementine's hand, afraid to move and awaken her. Her thoughts returned to the service she'd attended last night. They had sat in a circle, herself, the couple she'd walked in with, the pastor, and nine others. Whatever Helen had been expecting when she'd set out for the church from the hospital, this wasn't it. But she felt captured somehow, riding in a rowboat without oars down a river of events that was much greater than herself. The words the pastor had said as she'd placed her feet in the big metal basin echoed in her mind, washing over her again like the water from his pitcher. "Greater love has no one than this, that someone lay down his life for his friends."

Was that what love was? She watched Clementine, her face turned to the side on her starched pillow and her chest laboring with each fragile rise and fall.

It seemed to Helen that all of her life she'd avoided entanglements and commitments. She had let others go to the place of distress to comfort and assist, all in the name of freedom to live her life as she wanted. But what if those were the places where real life existed?

There was new territory here, here in the rumpled sheets of a hospital bed, here in the worn, needy face of someone who had spent her own life calming and comforting others, unselfishly doing her duty. Helen stood at the edge of it, but inside she knew that her course was already set. She knew too much of the path Clementine had already traveled to let her carry on alone.

Chapter 42

Clementine had a steady stream of visitors. Mrs. Leopold, Mr. Blanchet, and other tenants of the apartment building all came to see their friend. Cards and visitors also arrived from Clementine's parish. But no one was as faithful a visitor as Helen. Helen felt, and maybe for the first time, responsible for someone. Why she felt responsible for Clementine she wouldn't have been able to say. Neither, in all likelihood, would she have been able to articulate that that is what she felt. Nevertheless, the feeling pleased her and filled something inside, knowing that her actions, her work, truly mattered in the life of someone else. If God had sent her to Clementine's apartment at just the right time, she knew it must be for a purpose, and her job was not to try to figure out the *why* of the purpose but simply to act upon it.

So it wasn't all that surprising when at the end of ten days, the doctor spoke with her and she heard herself deciding to bring Clementine home with her.

"Miss Cavaziel is doing much, much better," said Dr. Solomon. "You are very dedicated to her even though you aren't related. I think that has helped her recover quickly."

"Yes, well, she has been very good to me," said Helen.

"She will be ready to leave in a few more days. I think now she mostly needs to get out of the hospital. But she still needs to be cared for; she can't be on her own. And I understand her apartment was ruined?"

"Yes, she can't go back there, it's not repaired yet."

There was a pause. Helen was thoughtful.

"She'll come home with me."

"Are you sure? She'll need round-the-clock care for a few more weeks, especially if this heat wave continues. Her lungs are stabilized, but they still need to heal, as much as they can. It would be possible for her to stay here."

He was giving her a way out, a way free from entanglement. A part of her wanted to grasp it, to escape, to keep veering away from commitment. But it was a part of her that was growing steadily smaller.

"Yes, I'm sure. She can stay with me."

***

At the office, Mr. Major was unhappy with Helen's request to take the following week off. She was already distracted in her work, consumed by the state of Clementine's health, leaving early to visit her or to help sort out her apartment. Everyone else had been nice enough about it though, glad that Helen was taking care of someone, who, while not a relative, was obviously someone important in her life.

"Don't worry, honey," said Pansy on Friday afternoon. "You just do what you need to do. The girls and I will all help pick up the slack while you're gone."

On Sunday afternoon Helen brought Clementine home with her by taxi. She had prepared her own room with fresh sheets on the bed, the still colorful zinnias and the latest edition of House Beautiful. Of course neither she nor Clementine had a house, but the newsstand hadn't had Vogue or Ladies' Home Journal. It was the closest she could find to the sort of design magazine that she thought Clementine might enjoy, so it would have to do for now.

She settled a reluctant Clementine into her own bed; she would sleep in Rose's room for the time being. Clementine was a good patient, talking little, sleeping a great deal, but even so, Helen found the task of being a caregiver all-consuming.

She decided to make meals that would tempt her patient, but since she had never been much of a cook she had a steep learning curve. No matter, she thought, as she pulled out a copy of *The Joy of Cooking* from the bottom shelf of her bedroom bookcase, now is obviously the time. It was a brand new copy, one of the wedding presents that had been left behind when she'd sailed for Germany as a new bride. The spine cracked as she opened it.

She should make chicken soup, she decided, to nourish the invalid. The temperatures had cooled somewhat; soup seemed less out of place at 80 degrees than 98. Helen had always thought she should learn how to make soup, anyway. In books making soup was always mentioned in such a casual way, as if people were born knowing how to make it. There was an aura about soup making, it seemed, a mysterious link to times past, grandmothers simmering things, and the collective memory of women. It intrigued Helen in a philosophical sense, but in the practical was part of the great unknown realm of cookery. Helen hadn't the slightest idea how to go about it, and she had nothing the recipe called for but an onion. As she wrote her shopping list and wondered what exactly a bay leaf was and what it was for, she heard a faint call from her bedroom. She dropped her pen onto the kitchen table with a smack and hurried to answer the call.

Clementine lay propped up on all the pillows in the apartment. She had been dozing when Helen had left her, but now her face registered a kind of panic.

"Rose isn't here, is she?" she asked faintly.

"No, she's not. She's with her parents down at the shore. She won't be back until week after next at the earliest."

Clementine nodded with relief and sank back down onto the pillows, but anxiety still showed in her eyes.

Chapter 43

Helen wondered if being a caregiver was anything like having a child. It was time-consuming work and sapped her energy, but to her surprise she found that she loved it. She was, in fact, for the first time learning to care more about someone else than herself. In the moments when Clementine was awake, Helen, wanting to keep Clementine's anxiety at bay, read her articles from the *Times* or asked questions about her childhood in the mountains.

Helen, in turn, told about her own childhood in Seattle—which felt bland in comparison—her family, and her time in Germany. With each bit of shared knowledge or experience, a thread stretched from one woman to another, something each felt beyond explanation or acknowledgment. Helen was faintly aware that something in her was changing, for the better she hoped. Maybe as a result of hearing about Clementine's life, she would become more like this woman who she realized she admired terribly.

Not that there was much time for self-reflection. During the times when Clementine rested, there was the washing to do and then the cooking. Following her now broken-in cookbook, she had succeeded in cooking chicken soup, a pork roast, and a beef stew that weren't terrible. Although Clementine's appetite was not great, she did her best to eat to reward Helen's efforts. Then there was the marketing, which she did at the small grocers in the neighborhood, fearing to leave Clementine on her own for very long.

There seemed to be countless little things to do now that someone was dependent on her, things that Helen had never noticed before. One would have thought she'd had this experience in Germany, with Heinrich, she thought to herself one day. A sudden pang of guilt seized her. She thought of herself back then. It really wasn't very long ago, but she was ashamed at how selfish the image in her memory was. She had never seen it before, but it was as though someone wiped a mirror clean, and she was amazed she had not seen it until now. Heinrich had been a difficult man, yes, described by a friend as a "typical dictatorial inflexible German," but what about her own part? Had she really tried? Had she even tried to love him? Not love the idea of who she thought he should be, but him, how he really was? Had she even considered who he really was? Had she ever once done something for him out of pure thoughtfulness? How much time had she ever spent thinking how to take care of him? Maybe the outcome would have been the same, but the thought struck her now that were she able to do it over again, she would have lived differently.

***

Rose returned home after Clementine had been there a week. She was very welcoming and courteous to Clementine, but since the patient was Helen's friend, Rose made no move to take over Helen's role as caregiver. In truth, perhaps Rose was gratified that for once Helen was the caregiver, instead of Helen needing Rose to fill that role. Helen, who had been sleeping in Rose's bed while Clementine slept in her own, now decamped to the living room sofa. And though Clementine looked uncomfortable and unwell when in Rose's presence, it didn't seem in any way suspicious; she really was unwell and uncomfortable. The relative tranquility of the previous week had disappeared, however; though not visibly or audibly, Helen could feel it. Rose's presence, though caring and pleasant, reminded Clementine of too many things left unspoken and undone.

For the first few days, Clementine and Rose hardly saw each other, but Helen sensed a determination on the part of her Swiss friend to get well and leave. Clementine became much more businesslike, more like her usual self.

"I will go soon, dear Helen," she said one afternoon when Rose was out. "You've been so very kind. But it's high time for me to be back in my place and out of your way."

Helen was doubtful. "I'm not sure you can get back in your own place, just yet, even if you were entirely well, which I don't think you are. I spoke with Mr. Blanchet yesterday, and things are still in quite a state. They've finally gotten the old boards out, but the plaster hasn't been replaced yet."

"Ohh....a little bit of work going on won't bother me. I will leave tomorrow or the next day."

"But it *will* bother you, or at least your lungs. That kind of dust is just what the doctor said to keep you away from. I really don't think you're strong enough yet." Helen felt uncertain. She was no nurse, but even she could see that a woman who could barely get across to the bathroom on her own wasn't ready to fend for herself in an apartment three flights up.

Clementine took a deep, long breath. Then another, as if testing the strength of her lungs. Then she spoke again, slowly. "It is too strange to be here. This is not my life; I shouldn't be here." Helen thought she understood. She came closer and sat on the edge of the bed, closer than she ever had. She opened her mouth to speak and then stopped. She felt so inadequate for this. *Please help me, God*, she breathed, *give me words.*

"She is glad you are here. You are my friend, and Rose is grateful I can help you. I haven't said anything to her, and I won't as long as you don't want me to." Helen tried to sound convincing and comforting.

Clementine was quiet now, appeased for the moment, but when Rose came in to greet Clementine as she usually did when she got home, Helen saw the discomfort in her entire body. Clementine gave a pained smile and nod, and just barely glanced up at Rose, hardly trusting herself to catch Rose's eyes. Rose was too kind, or else too preoccupied, to see that her presence made the older woman so ill at ease.

"I hope you felt a little better today, Miss Clementine?" she asked.

"Yes, fine, fine, always a little better," Clementine answered, staring down and fussing with her blanket.

Later, Rose and Helen sat quietly together in the living room. Rose's parents had sent her home from vacation with a television set.

"You can't ignore technology; it will keep changing whether you like it or not," Mr. Whitaker had said. "Even I know that, and I'm a Luddite if there ever was one. Besides now you can watch the Ed Sullivan show and know what everyone is talking about."

They had now switched the machine on and were quietly watching the black-and-white figures moving around inside the little box. Rose turned from where she was curled up in the corner of the couch and spoke.

"Clementine says she is doing better, Helen, but do you think she really is? She seems very weak to me."

"I'm not sure what to think. She really isn't better, but she wants to go home as soon as possible."

They spoke in near whispers, so as not to be heard from the other room. Helen got up and turned up the volume slightly on the set.

"I haven't really had a chance to ask you if you minded a guest, Rose. Do you? I really haven't got a good idea how much longer it will be, but I know she isn't ready to be on her own yet."

"And she doesn't have any family?" As she looked at her, Helen felt Rose would surely read the secret in her own gaze.

"No." She paused. "They are all in Switzerland...she never married," she added as an afterthought.

"Well, I don't mind her staying at all. She seems like a wonderful person, and I feel just awful that the accident happened while she was working on my dress." She looked up quickly. "Not for the dress, mind you, I don't care about that, I just feel terrible that she felt like she had to be working on it on the hottest day of the year. I hope she didn't feel that kind of pressure from me or Mother."

"No, Rose, I think she was eager to work on it for her own reasons. She really wants it to be something special."

They sat quietly for a minute, the television droning mindlessly on, but neither listening, each absorbed in her own thoughts.

"You know, Helen," said Rose finally, "this is good for you, somehow. It's really lovely to see the way you care for her."

"Thank you," said Helen simply. She felt it, too, something moving inside her, some center of gravity shifting. She felt it, and liked it, but had no words to describe it.

They were companionably quiet again for a moment.

"And your work? The Committee's been alright with you taking so much time off?"

"Well, they're not thrilled, but they seem to be surviving without me."

In fact, Pansy had called again that afternoon to convey the sentiment from Mr. Major that The Committee was anxious for Helen's return. "Of course everyone understands that you're taking care of this lady, but honestly, Helen, hadn't you better make some other arrangements? With her family or something? Because, in my opinion, Mr. Major has been pretty patient with you, but his patience is maybe wearing thin. The girls and I are trying hard to cover for you, but there's only so much we can do."

After she'd hung up, Helen thought about Pansy's last sentence. Had she been mistaken in thinking that Pansy's voice had had a bit of an edge to it?

Ivan called as well. Was she interested in another dinner date?

"It's so awfully nice of you to ask, but just now I'm taking care of my friend who is sick."

"Oh yes, I heard about something like that." He said it in the tone of a man who knows when he is being put off.

"Ivan, I really would like to go out with you. I mean it. It's just that this week isn't possible; I can't leave my friend alone. Maybe in a couple weeks?"

"Of course, Helen." He didn't sound convinced. "I will call in a few weeks."

"Thank you, Ivan. For understanding."

"It is not a problem, Helen." His voice was heavy and cool.

With a sting of shame, she recalled how she had treated Ivan last autumn. She wished she could find the words to say something else, to convey to him that she wasn't that person anymore. To say that it was not a mistake to call her again, it would be worth it to give her a second chance.

"Well, thank you then for the call. I'll talk to you in a few weeks?"

"Yes. Goodbye, Helen."

"Um, bye...Ivan."

The only person Helen really would have really liked to talk to did not call. She did not want to admit it to herself, but it was Thomas she wanted to speak to. But it was more of a vague desire than a well-thought-out wish. She wanted his approval, she wanted him to see her with Clementine. Not so she could boast, but so he could see how she had changed, softened. When she'd cooked a pot roast with moderate success the other night, her thoughts had turned fleetingly to him, wishing he could taste it. She was almost angry with herself, at her need for some sort of approval of her cooking skills by a man.

But it isn't like that, she thought in the next moment. *Thomas is my friend, and friends enjoy bringing delight to their friends.* Thomas was her friend. Thomas was her *friend.* It struck her in an odd way suddenly. Was that what was different with him? Was that why mere thoughts of him made her want to be a better person? He was her *friend.* This was uncharted land. No one, no man, not Heinrich, not Vladimir, not anyone else had ever been a true friend, getting to know her, wanting the best for her, wanting her to become everything she wanted to be, but at the same time wanting her just the way she was.

She would write to him. When Thomas had left, she hadn't thought it possible. She didn't think it would matter so much to her. Now she knew. He did mean that much.

He meant everything.

She would write to him tonight when Clementine was asleep and the apartment was quiet after dinner.

Chapter 44

Fred was joining them for supper. Helen, growing confident, roasted a chicken with a lemon rosemary stuffing, and Rose made a green salad. It was a big outing for Clementine to come to the table, and when the meal was ready, Helen helped her walk slowly from her bedroom. She sat quietly at the table across from Fred, while Rose and Helen sat at the table ends. As Helen brought the chicken and roast potatoes to the table, she saw Clementine glancing cautiously toward Rose, then away again. Rose was quiet as well, her chin in her hand and her elbow leaning on the table, a smile playing over her face as she listened to Fred. Fred was unusually animated and carried the conversation for most of the evening, which Helen thought was an excellent thing, under the circumstances.

"I've had another director take a look at *Chaff in the Wind*," he said as Helen filled his plate.

"What good news!" said Helen.

"Yes, and this director has done a lot of similar plays, so I think there's a good chance this may be the one." He glanced at Rose who smiled at him even more broadly.

"And what did he say?" asked Helen.

"Well," Fred looked down at his hands, then up at Helen who was finishing serving up. "He's only just gotten it, so he hasn't told me anything yet. But it shouldn't be too long."

There was a quiet pause, and Clementine made her way to fill it. Her voice, unused and still recovering, was thin and willowy.

"What is your play about, Fred?"

"It's a musical actually," he began in a voice as soft as hers. Then he grinned at himself, and started again more excitedly. "They're coming back in fashion, you know, musicals are. Look at *My Fair Lady*." Then Fred scratched the back of his graying head and looked down at his napkin. "It's about my family, my grandparents actually, who were farmers in Minnesota. They were immigrants who came here from Norway with nothing and built their life and family through hard work. There's lots of struggles of course, but it's all about how the love of family pulls you through those."

Helen was dishing a slice of chicken onto Clementine's plate, and looked up discreetly to see her reaction. Clementine was nodding slightly, a thoughtful look on her face.

"And it has a happy ending, the story?" she asked.

"Of course! If a musical has a sad ending, doesn't that make it an opera?" he said and then laughed at his own joke.

"I'm certain it's going to be a huge success," said Rose. "It just needs the right director, and now, with any luck, Fred's got him." Fred beamed at her and took her hand in his.

"Well," said Helen breezily, "Bon appétit!"

They ate quietly for a while. The roast chicken had turned out well, and Helen was pleased. Done enough and taken out just before it got too dry. With a gracious nod she accepted the compliments that came from all sides of the table.

"Speaking of family, Fred survived his stay with mine last week."

"More than survived, I'd say. Passed with flying colors. Mr. Whitaker took me out fishing, and I caught a fish right away. A cod or mackerel or something. Anyway, it tasted good, and it brought me honor, thank heavens. I did not shame my dear Rose."

"Daddy was quite proud of him, and kept telling all the neighbors about his future son-in-law who'd caught something his first time out fishing."

"It does mean a lot to me, actually. Family is really important to me, to us. The most important thing." He looked at Rose and she gazed back at him. Their eyes held a moment, and Helen tried not to be sick. She wondered how all the talk of family was going over with Clementine. She looked at her.

"Clementine, are you feeling alright? You look very pale. Maybe it's time to get you back to bed," Helen gently suggested, offering her an escape.

"I'm sorry, yes I think I should go. I do feel not quite right."

"I can bring your dessert to you there, if you like."

"No, thank you, Helen. I don't want to eat anymore."

Chapter 45

The next day, Helen went out to Carpenter's Grocery when she thought Clementine would be resting. As she rounded the corner at Madison, on her way back home, Angelo walked quickly down the sidewalk to meet her. His face was flushed and worried.

"Miss Hartmann! Your friend, Miss Clementine, she comes down the elevator and then she faints right in the lobby!"

"What?" cried Helen.

"Yes! I don't know why she's tryin' to walk around now. She's not well enough yet, I don't think."

"Where is she, Angelo?"

"She's on the chair in my room. She's okay for right now, but I been lookin' for you, waitin' til you get home."

Clementine was slumped on a brown vinyl chair, half asleep and very pale. Her chest rose and fell irregularly and Helen pursed her lips together and willed herself not to panic. With Angelo's help, Helen got her in the elevator and back upstairs to the apartment. Clementine hardly responded to

Helen's attempts at comforting words and didn't offer any explanation as Helen gently questioned her motive. Over her face lay a mask of indifference, only her eyes showed her sadness and frustration.

***

"She's obviously had a setback," said Dr. Solomon. "Her lungs sound like they've improved, but her whole state of health is very weak. She somehow seems like a much older woman than she really is."

Helen listened and nodded as the doctor spoke quietly. They stood in her living room. He had made a house call to spare Clementine the effort of traveling.

"She said she wanted to go home, that she didn't want to trouble you anymore. That was her reason for leaving. And a foolish one. The collapse has done damage to the progress she'd made. She'll need to stay here even longer, I'm afraid, and be kept as calm as possible. Or we could move her back to the hospital. I've prescribed more sedatives."

"It's alright. I want her to stay until she's really better. And my roommate does, too. I can't understand why she felt she had to leave," Helen said, although it wasn't exactly true. She had a strong suspicion why.

The doctor peered at Helen through his owlish glasses. "Well, I have a hunch that there's something going on that's not just physical. But that isn't my department, so I can only wish you the best of luck. You know how to reach me." With that, he picked up his hat and case and left.

***

"I can't stay any longer, dear Helen. You've been too kind, but I really don't belong here," said Clementine with a weak smile.

"Yes, you do, Clementine," said Helen. "You are my friend, and friends care for each other."

Clementine just sighed into her pillow.

"It just seems so pointless now, my life. Never able to leave here again because of...because of her. I suppose always hoping somehow, always wanting it to be different. But now I see her, I see her life, her family, and I have no place here. She doesn't need me at all, and it's better if she doesn't. And then I think, what have I been doing all this time then? What a waste it's been."

Helen had no idea how to answer and instead reached behind Clementine's head for her pillow. She fluffed it up and turned it so the cool side was up.

"You just need rest," she said lamely. "You should take your medicine again now."

"I don't need rest. Rest only makes me think even more. I just want to forget." But she pushed herself up and swallowed the green pill that Helen held out in one hand, a glass of water in the other. "I just want to go to sleep forever." She leaned back onto her pillow and closed her eyes with a heavy sigh.

Helen set down the glass of water on the bedside table next to the box of sleeping pills. She looked at Clementine lying still and quiet and then back to the box. She reached and picked it up again without a sound, and walked out to the kitchen. She opened the cupboard above the refrigerator and slid the small green box behind a carton of Cream of Wheat.

Late that evening, Helen sat with Rose on their blue sofa in the living room. She had liked the sofa so much when she'd found it secondhand. Its sleek modern lines seemed such a statement, a farewell to all the antiques she'd grown up with in her parents' home and all the traditional ornate furniture she'd seen in Germany. But sitting here how, she had to admit that all its angles were hard and uncomfortable.

Fred had stopped in for a brief visit and had just left. Now the two women sat, Helen with her stockinged feet stretched out to the coffee table and Rose with hers stretched out along the sofa, a yellow velvet pillow wedged behind her back and the stupidly low arm of the sofa. She was half turned to face Helen.

"Maybe she just feels too much like your project. She seems like quite an independent woman. It must be hard to feel so out of control when you're used to having your life in order."

"Yes," said Helen. She was quiet. She thought about the woman, her friend, who lay sleeping fitfully on her own bed. She thought about the promise she'd made her, and she thought about what kinds of circumstances released you from promises. She looked long and hard at Rose, who looked back at her placidly. The lamp behind her made the edges of her dark curls stand out. In her green eyes shone the constant contentment Helen saw when Rose was around Fred. It was a look she was sure no one had ever seen in her own eyes when she was with Heinrich. She wondered for a moment if her eyes would ever hold that kind of look, whether it was something everyone could have, or whether it was only for some. She wondered if it came back after someone had disrupted that deep calm. Helen shifted and pulled her legs back underneath her on the dreadful couch. She took a deep breath.

"Rose," she said. Her voice was strained. This was not at all how she had once imagined it. "There's something I need to tell you."

Chapter 46

Rose left early the next morning without a word to Helen. She had become very upset during the conversation with Helen, first by the suggestion she made, and then by the possibility that it could be true.

"It's ludicrous, Helen. You read too many novels."

"But don't you see? They both knew your aunt's friend, Sister Felicity. It's not actually all that ludicrous. Highly unlikely, maybe, but not impossible."

Rose couldn't argue. She grew more uncomfortable as Helen continued with all the details and facts she'd kept tallied in her mind for so long, especially the birthday that came just when the roses came into bloom. Rose was the most agitated Helen had ever seen her. She kept shifting on the sofa until she was sitting bolt upright. Her jaw was jutted out and she kept opening and closing her mouth. Finally Helen was silent.

Then after a moment she said, "You know, Rose, she wanted to do what was best for you. For her baby."

At that, Rose got up abruptly and walked to her bedroom.

"Goodnight, Helen," she said, closing the door. The next morning she was gone.

***

On Saturday afternoon, Clementine finally roused. For two days she'd done almost nothing but sleep, helped by the doctor's little green pills. Her face looked a little less drawn than it had.

"What day is it, Helen?" she asked her friend when she was sitting up in bed, drinking orange juice out of the petite green tumbler. Helen was glad Clementine had slept so well. It helped make up for her own lack of sleep; she'd spent the last two nights tossing and turning, wondering if she'd done the right thing.

"Saturday," answered Helen.

"And what day of the month? I've lost all track of time, I'm afraid." Her voice seemed infinitesimally stronger and very groggy.

"Me too," Helen said, "I'll go look."

Helen walked to the kitchen to the wall calendar hanging there. Her mother had gotten it free from the bank and sent it on to her. Mount Rainier Mutual Bank was written in bold at the top of a color photo of a snowy mountain. The tear-off pages were stapled below. Helen had lost track of the days sometime last week, each one bleeding into the next, all care and soup making and temperature taking. Now August's page hung on the calendar, but that couldn't be right. Around the 1st on the calendar was drawn a circle in red pencil. Helen had drawn it ages ago—felt like years ago—to mark the decision date Thomas had given her, the beginning of August. At the time, she'd marked it more out of obligation, not thinking it would really have meaning for her, and it had seemed an eternity away. Now it stared her in the face. She had no memory of tearing off the page of July. She thought for a moment. She hadn't. Rose must have torn off the last month two days ago.

Helen swallowed hard and thought. If it was already August, and she wasn't entirely convinced it was, and it was Saturday, it must be the 3rd. August 3rd. She walked slowly back to the bedroom.

"It's August 3rd," she told Clementine.

Clementine looked at her a long moment through her glasses.

"August already?"

"I can hardly believe it myself. We lost track of time in all this, I guess."

Clementine looked up at her sleepily, at Helen who had lost track of time in caring for her, and smiled. A beautiful, peaceful smile. Helen smiled back, happy at Clementine's happiness. They both laughed softly together. Then Helen, still smiling, pressed her lips together and turned away.

***

Standing in the kitchen later, Helen stared at the calendar again as though it had deceived her. She had since checked in her own personal diary and gone out to the newsstand and bought today's *Times* to confirm the date. The beginning of August had come and gone and she had missed Thomas' deadline. And the letter that she had decided to write him had been begun, but then forgotten in Clementine's setback. All at once, she enflamed with anger. What right did he have to impose deadlines on her? What kind of a relationship was that? What kind of controlling personality did that reveal? Even as the thoughts flashed through her mind, she thought of Thomas and how he had looked at her just before he said anything at all about August. His honest, unpretentious face. His smiling eyes gone all serious. He truly cared about her. She knew he truly loved her. *If what you want is me, then I am a happy, happy man. And if you don't, then the sooner I know that for sure the better.*

He'd been kind, she knew, patient with her, and a date on the calendar had just been one more kindness. He'd been willing to wait until now to move on with his life, beginning up there in Deerfield, Massachusetts. He'd been willing to wait, and now he had his answer and he would move on without her. She imagined him somewhere vaguely up north, surrounded by green fields and deer, with an enormous book in front of him, turning some giant page, ready to step onto a new one. She laughed in spite of herself at the image. Even from this distance, Thomas made her laugh. She laughed and the tears rolled down her cheeks.

She thought of trying to call him to explain. It was still the beginning of August, wasn't it? It was only the 3rd after all. The 3rd was not the 25th. But as she thought it, she knew she wouldn't. That had been the whole point, hadn't it?

That she couldn't make up her mind, couldn't stay focused, that she didn't know what she wanted. That had been just what had frustrated Thomas, and why he had bothered mentioning a date at all. She couldn't call. It would just be one more piece of evidence for him that she hadn't wanted him badly enough, hadn't cared enough before.

When Rose came back Monday afternoon, Helen was grateful that her roommate was too preoccupied to notice her own feelings. Rose came in, went quickly to her room and put down her bag and came back to where Helen was in the kitchen a few minutes later.

"Is Clementine in your room?" she said.

"Yes," said Helen. She had left her reading a magazine a few moments before.

Rose looked at Helen a long moment without saying anything. Then she took a deep breath and turned and walked to the bedroom. Helen stood leaning against the kitchen counter a long time, unsure if she should go in and explain why she broke her promise to Clementine. She heard voices from the bedroom and her ears strained to pick up syllables, but Rose had closed the door. But they weren't angry voices, so for the time being she would leave them alone. She had imagined this moment long ago, with herself in the center of it, emanating a rosy glow like an angel in a medieval painting. Now she was not in the center of the moment, and what she mostly felt was anxiety. For Rose, for Clementine. So she went for a walk.

Angelo opened the door downstairs.

"Everything good today, Miss Hartmann?"

"Yes, Angelo, thank you. Miss Cavaziel is doing better now, I think. I'm just going for a little walk."

"Ah, that's good...You been doing nothin' but taking care of her. She's a nice lady, but you gotta take care of yourself too. You take some time for yourself."

Helen turned and looked at Angelo. His broad honest face, his dark eyes showing concern for her, actually caring about her when she hardly knew more of him than his name and his accent.

"I think my problem is that I've always taken time for myself."

Angelo's dark eyes looked puzzled, so Helen smiled a big, full smile just to show she was alright. Then she started walking along 92nd Street.

When Helen came back, hours later, she found Rose and Clementine still together in the now-open bedroom. Rose had made tea for the two of them and pulled the armchair up close to the bedside. When Helen peeked in, they both looked up quickly and sheepishly, like high schoolers out on a first date. Helen smiled and felt awkward herself. She backed out and let them resume their talk, which she could only imagine was each woman retelling her story for the one person on Earth who wanted to hear it most.

Helen made some ham sandwiches and brought a plate of them to the bedroom. They thanked her, but still looked sheepish, so she left and went to eat her own sandwich on the couch. After she'd finished eating, she tidied the kitchen and then vacuumed the living room. After that, she wasn't sure what she should do. She turned on the television quietly and watched a little bit, the stories of other people's lives a welcome escape from thinking about her own.

Chapter 47

In the morning she called the office. It was time, she thought, for her to go back to work. Clementine looked like a different person, not speaking much to Helen, but with color in her face and a light in her eyes. She was certainly healing more quickly; now she had a reason to. Clementine needed to stay at Helen and Rose's a little longer, but she would be fine while Helen was at work.

Lily, one of the junior secretaries, answered her call. "Um...I'll have Pansy call you back in a little while, okay Helen? She's a little busy at the moment."

But Pansy didn't call back, so Helen tried again in the afternoon, with the same result. Finally she called just before five o'clock.

"Hello again, Lily, isn't Pansy there?"

"No, um, she's here. It's just...well, it's a little complicated. I'll see if she can talk to you right now."

Pansy came on the line, sounding winded and important.

"Oh, hi, Helen! Hey, I've missed you. Listen, I've got to go take a memo that's really priority, so I'll call you back first thing tomorrow morning, okay?"

Before Helen could answer, Pansy continued, "Alrighty then, bye!"

The next morning Pansy called as she said she would, but her voice was far from her usual swingy self. She was businesslike and to-the-point.

"The thing is, Helen, is that when it really seemed like you didn't care about your job anymore, Mr. Major got fed up and gave it to someone else."

Helen's mouth went dry. Her palms were damp and she shifted the telephone receiver to the other ear.

"Wha – who did he give it to? Who's got my job?" she said as she found her voice.

There was a pause on the other end of the line. "Well... me, actually," said Pansy.

There was a long silence. Then Helen began to splutter.

"But how could he...how could you...? Why didn't anybody tell me?"

"Well, honey, we tried to, but you weren't being real communicative yourself, if you remember. And Mr. Major's a busy man. He's got the freedom of the West at stake. He doesn't really have time to go running after everybody and their old Swedish relatives or whatever."

Helen swallowed. The lump in her throat hurt her. "She's Swiss. Can I talk to him?" Her voice sounded wooden in her ears.

"Well, okay, if you want to. I'm not sure that's gonna help or anything, but if it makes you feel better. He'll be around tomorrow morning."

Helen hung up the phone, sure that there was some mistake. Mr. Major was a busy man, but not an unjust one. He would have at least made it clear what the stakes were before letting her go. She would go in tomorrow and find out.

So she went the next morning, dressed up in her office best, as she hadn't been for what felt like months rather than weeks. The air on the subway felt stifling, even though it was not as full as usual. Many of the regular commuters had taken part of August off to get out of the city.

Lily and the other secretaries seemed genuinely pleased to see her, but as they exchanged greetings and pleasantries they glanced nervously in the direction of Mr. Major's office and Helen's desk. As Helen walked over, Pansy was just coming out of Mr. Major's office. She closed the door, then glanced up and took in the room. Upon seeing Helen's approach, she began shuffling papers in her hand and sat down importantly in Helen's chair. She looked up again, very quickly, but her face gave nothing away.

"Hello, Helen. You look nice. Mr. Major's actually free and can talk to you right now." She held up her arm, palm up, in the direction of Mr. Major's door, as if Helen didn't know where it was. As Helen moved in that direction, Pansy stood up again brusquely and opened the door.

"It's Helen Hartmann, sir," she chirped as she ushered Helen in. Then she disappeared and shut the door.

"AH, Helen!" said Mr. Major. His voice was large and projected more than it needed to inside his office, as if he were trying to broadcast behind the Iron Curtain directly from here. "I'm *so* sorry to hear about your grandmother. Glad you've been able to help her out. I hope she's doing better now?"

"Uh, yes, sir," said Helen, though for an instant she was puzzled what her grandmother had to do with anything.

He came around his desk and put his arm briefly on her shoulder. It was meant to be kind, a sort of condolence for her sick grandmother, but to Helen, the weight of it, even for the second it was there, felt more like a threat. Helen wasn't sure how to begin on the topic at hand. She opened her mouth to speak, but Mr. Major beat her to it. He was already moving back around his desk, on the other side this time.

"The thing is, things don't stand still around here, do they? Even for sick grandmothers." He laughed at his own remark, a loud burst of guffaw. "Things move along and so do we. So I'm sorry about your spot." He spoke as if it were a seat on the bus.

"It's just that I don't understand why you wouldn't give me some idea, some...notice." *Before giving me notice*, she thought.

"But we did! And when Pansy told us that you'd said you were no longer interested, we figured that implied your decision."

"But I told her no such thing, sir!" said Helen. She was flabbergasted, her breath coming in short gasps.

Mr. Major rumpled his forehead and pushed his lips out. He leaned back in his swivel chair and crossed one leg over the other. "Well then, that's too bad." For a second Helen had a hope that he saw the injustice of the situation. But the moment passed, and he had already moved on. "But what's done is done, and now we have to keep moving, you know?" He certainly kept moving, his upper foot wiggling and twitching, full of nervous energy. He sat up at his desk again and looked down at the papers that covered it. His side of the conversation seemed to be over.

Helen felt deflated. She almost turned to go out right then, without saying a word. But in her mind she could hear Thomas' voice. *Be persistent. Don't give up without trying.*

"But, sir," she said. "I love my job, and I believe in The Committee. There was a mistake, a miscommunication, and I don't want to leave. I never wanted to leave for good." She was glad to hear in her own voice an edge of determination. Mr. Major heard it, too.

He stopped wiggling and jiggling and looked straight at her for a moment, silently.

"Helen, you're a good girl and good at your job. The Committee loves you. But I can't give you your old job back, that wouldn't be fair to Pansy now would it? But maybe if you like, you could work with some of the other secretaries in the pool. You'll have to go talk to Mrs. Hanson about it. Yes, that would be good, talk to Mrs. Hanson." He paused, then swung his hands together and started fidgeting again. "Good luck, Helen," he said with a nod and then turned back to protecting the freedoms of the West.

Mrs. Hanson, Mrs. Hanson. Helen knew what that meant. She could come back at the very bottom. She moved stiffly out of the office, closing the door behind her. Pansy was at her typewriter, tapping briskly away. Her work was so important she couldn't look up. Helen didn't want to look Pansy in the face, but as she passed she could feel Pansy's eyes slanting her direction.

Helen whispered loudly, "You told him I didn't want my job?!"

"Well, that's what you told me, sweetie." Her voice was all syrupy and sweetness.

"I did no such thing, Pansy!"

"I called and I called, but you never had any time to talk about it. In the end, Mr. Major needed a replacement for you, and...I was available." She dragged the last part of her sentence out, and now Helen could see the faintest trace of a smile on the edge of her lips. It was smug.

"So, it's too bad, I guess, Helen. But you'll give Mrs. Hanson a call, won't you?" She pulled the paper out of the typewriter loudly and turned to carry it off somewhere. Somewhere surely very important. Helen walked away.

On the way home, she had the idea of calling Ivan. She had promised to call him anyway, and maybe, just maybe, he could have a little influence. Thinking about it all now, she wasn't sure she wanted to work for someone who had cast her aside with so little pretense, or that she wanted to make Pansy move aside forcibly. She knew Pansy and knew she would not take that easily. She had always been ambitious and now Helen had seen just how far that ambition had gone. Helen felt stupid for not seeing it before and for not having done better at protecting her own job. Now that she thought about it, it seemed like Ivan had sort of always known that, had maybe wanted to protect Helen from Pansy in a way. He really was a very decent guy.

She recalled a year ago, giggling with Pansy and calling him Ivan the Terrible. Pansy had called him that first, she was sure. If not for her, she would have seen long ago what a nice fellow he was. Her anger flaring, she seemed to see that Pansy was to blame for everything that wasn't working in her life. She was almost ready to blame her for Thomas moving away. But no, she knew that wasn't right and wasn't just. There, Pansy was in no way involved and that was a good thing.

Once home, she dialed Ivan's home number. It rang and rang and then gave a funny click before the line gave way to nothing. An operator came on the line, her voice metallic and slow.

"I'm sorry but that number seems to have been disconnected. May I help you?"

"No, no," said Helen uncertainly and hung up. It was odd. With a start, she realized that Ivan would still be at work, anyway, it was still an office day. She dialed The Committee's main number.

"American Committee," answered a young female voice.

"Ivan Kolovskov, please."

"I'm sorry, Ma'am, Mr. Kolovskov is no longer in this office. May I help you?"

"Lily?" asked Helen. She was almost sure it was her. "Lily, it's Helen. What do you mean? Where's Ivan?"

"Oh, Helen! I'm so sorry about what happened. At least, I'm not quite sure exactly what happened, but you didn't look too happy when you left today."

"That's kind, Lily. But what happened to Ivan?"

"Oh, right! Didn't you hear? He's being transferred to the Munich bureau, and he's already gone ahead to arrange things."

"He's left?" Her voice had an uncomfortable squeak in it.

"Yes. He got promoted to chief of the Hungary section. It all happened pretty suddenly, but he seemed really glad about the chance to move on. He left last week." She paused, listening for Helen, but Helen was quiet, totally unsure what to say. "Do you want me to get a message to him? I can send one inside mail, if you like. I think he'll be back before the end of the month to close up his apartment."

"No, no, it's alright. Thanks, though. I guess it's not that important. It can wait."

"Well, alright then, Helen. Good luck! Will we see you around here again soon?"

"Oh, sure," Helen said pleasantly, but she knew the answer was no.

Chapter 48

Clementine and Rose were getting along well. Extremely well. Almost too well. Even Helen, who had imagined all this in sunshiny fantasy images, was surprised at just how much time they spent together chatting. Clementine moved out to the sofa during the day, and looked healthier each morning. Rose had some work to do at the school to prepare for the coming school year, but she still had a large amount of free time to spend with Clementine, recounting her childhood and listening to Clementine recount hers. After the initial tension, the awkwardness of their new relationship seemed to fade away, and when Rose talked about Clementine to Helen, Helen thought she sensed a new strain of compassion in Rose's voice. Clementine needed less real care now. Mostly she seemed to need companionship and conversation. Helen was grateful that Rose carried the bulk of the conversations as her own thoughts were jumbled and messy inside her.

One day Rose asked Helen how she was doing. Helen hadn't been completely honest about the situation at work, but Rose was perceptive enough to know that all was not well.

"And how's Thomas? Do you have any news from him?"

"No," answered Helen a little too quickly. "No…," she continued more slowly, "but I don't really think he'd want to talk to me. Now."

Rose looked at her a long uncomfortable moment. Helen felt tears spring to her eyes and turned away.

***

On a Wednesday in mid-August, Helen sat alone on the apartment terrace. The days had taken an autumnal turn. Although still warm, they were gradually growing shorter. It made for long twilit evenings, which Helen loved and which seemed to fit her current melancholy. This evening Fred had come over, and he and Rose had taken Clementine for a walk over to Central Park. It was the second such outing, as Clementine seemed to grow stronger each day and more like her old self, or rather her old self transformed. The plan was to move her back to her own apartment the coming weekend. It was now repaired and prepared; Helen had gone down to see. After all, she didn't have much else to do. She had no job, she had no romantic prospects, and her patient was almost well and almost thoroughly attached to someone else. Helen swirled the wine in her glass and gazed out over the rooftops of New York. New York. What promise and mystery and freedom those words had held just twelve months ago. Freedom. That was what she had wanted most of all. Freedom from the past, freedom from tradition, freedom from the choices and entanglements she had made. And now, here she sat, in absolute freedom, alone and lonely.

She stood up. Suddenly she couldn't, wouldn't sit still. If only she could move fast enough to leave such thoughts behind. She went inside, grabbed her cardigan from off the chair, and quickly left the apartment. She barely nodded a response to Angelo's friendly greeting. At Madison she turned and walked north. Up the avenue she strode, determined, barely noticing the shops and people she passed, glad for the long twilight to hide her face. At 97th she crossed the street and turned west again, toward Central Park, with each stride breathing a little easier. The temperature was perfect, the day's heat finally dissipating into the cool of the evening. The cardigan was superfluous, and it swung from her hand.

At the intersection she stood and waited for the flow of cars to stop at the red light. She looked down the broad ease of 5th Avenue, the buses and taxis of the last commuters ambling north and groups of slowly meandering pedestrians scattered on the sidewalks of both sides of the street. It seemed that all the world was out enjoying the leafy greenness of the evening. Helen waited at the intersection for the light to change. The sudden sound of laughter made Helen look up at a group crossing back across the broad avenue. It was Rose and Fred, supporting Clementine walking between them. Her steps were slow, but steady. Rose and Clementine had their faces turned toward each other, both evidently giggling at some remark Fred had made. Fred was trying without success to keep a straight face. Helen shrank back a little behind the lamp post. But it was unnecessary; the little group was completely self-absorbed, a tiny community unto itself. Watching them progress steadily across the intersection, Helen felt something like a knife slicing across her heart. She was happy for them, wasn't she? It was what she had wanted for each of them. Clementine had found her daughter in flesh and blood, and no longer had to simply imagine her. Rose had found the woman who had given her life, and was slowly learning what that meant and how to build a relationship based on the fact that Clementine had given her up, not out of simple abandonment, but out of love.

With the hand that wasn't supporting Clementine, Rose pushed a dark curl out of her eyes and looked across at Fred. They smiled at each other, the smile of complicity in contentment. It was Fred, Helen had noticed, who initiated the most interaction with Clementine, as if Rose still needed an intermediary as she felt her way through this new relationship. The past few weeks had shown a side of Fred that Helen admired and respected. He was nurturing, protective of Rose's feelings, yet he encouraged her to show care for Clementine.

No one in the trio looked in Helen's direction. For the first time ever, Helen envied Rose. The two people next to her adored her and cared for her. Her parents in Connecticut loved her unconditionally. Her students and colleagues at the school admired and respected her. She had people to whom she belonged. Was she free? Maybe not in the way Helen had always understood freedom, but the bonds that held her were the threads of a netting of love. Perhaps, thought Helen, there could be a place of freedom somewhere in the center of all those bonds of community, of love, of commitment. The thought startled her, and she felt more alone than she had ever felt, since leaving Heinrich, since Vladimir, since Thomas had left, since the time she was a little girl, waiting—always waiting—for her parents to find the time to listen to her.

The light changed. Helen crossed over to the park. Looking westward she saw thunderclouds had mounted up and were quickly approaching. The first huge drops began to fall before she'd walked five minutes. Then faster and thicker they fell, in straight lines from the sky as thunder rolled heavily and the downpour increased. Helen pulled her cardigan feebly around her shoulders, as if to protect herself from the storm. But the air was still warm, and drenched as she was, she continued on past the reservoir and walked and walked and walked.

Chapter 49

Saturday afternoon Clementine moved back into her apartment. Mr. Blanchet carried up Miss Cavaziel's two small bags while she made her way slowly up the stairs supported by Helen on one side and Fred on the other. The apartment was clean and bright and smelled of nothing but fresh paint and the bouquet of yellow roses that Mrs. Leopold had brought. Clementine seemed very content to be back in her home, and after Helen had made a pot of tea and they all sat around drinking it awhile, it was time to leave. Mrs. Leopold promised to bring supper up to her neighbor and to keep an eye on her.

"I'll call tomorrow and see if you need anything," said Helen in parting.

"Oh, Helen, Mr. Blanchet here said he'd help me with groceries until I'm myself again. I'll be fine. You've done so much, and I'll be ever grateful. But now, dear, it's time for you to get on with your own life."

Back home that evening, sitting on the edge of her own bed, Clementine's words haunted her. It was time for her to get on with her own life. What on earth did that mean? Settling Clementine back in at home had been the last distraction to keep her from thinking about what a mess she'd made of her life. She felt like one of the paper boats children floated on the reservoir, rudderless and meandering with every ripple and eddy they came across. What on earth should she do now?

She thought again of the words of the preacher at Thomas' church. Is this what it meant to lay down your life for your friend, she wondered? What if you lay it down, and then when you go to pick it back up there's nothing left? Then what?

Helen made herself another cup of tea and wandered out to sit on the uncomfortable couch. It was still summer and the windows were open, but on the breeze came a freshness that foretold September. The prospect of Mrs. Hanson rose before her. She could always still call. But next to Mrs. Hanson rose an image of Pansy's smug smiling face and she knew she couldn't ever. Helen felt defeated, but not without dignity. No, she wouldn't stoop that low. Another job? She thought she could get a decent reference from Mr. Major, even though the subject of her reason for leaving would be a tricky one. Maybe she should just give it all up and begin something new.

Maybe, she thought suddenly, maybe she could learn sewing from Clementine and become a seamstress. For a moment she had a vision of herself working alongside Clementine, letting her become a sort of mother figure, imagining herself replacing Rose once again as the object of Clementine's affection. At the same time that her conscience rebelled against such a vision, reality did too. She remembered her mother showing her again and again how to lengthen a hem or work a buttonhole. It had never seemed to stick in her mind, and her fingers were clumsy next to her mother's quick agile ones. Working with Clementine was a lovely picture, but only that.

Thinking of her mother brought other images of her parents to mind. Reserved and thoughtful, never asking too many questions, never requiring too much. Her mother buttoning up her coat and checking in the hallway mirror to make sure her hat sat perfectly before leaving for work at the school. Her Daddy coming home from work at city hall, changing into overalls and going straight out to his garden. He was proud of his garden and especially his sweet corn. When the sweet corn was ripe he refused to pick the ears off the stalk until the water in the kitchen was boiling.

She had thought, too, of going back home to her parents and letting them take care of her. She knew they would, with few questions and trying hard to hide their disappointment in her. From this distance and with her recent failures, the simplicity of their life appealed to her, each day as regular and similar as the one before. On Sundays they walked down to church, and in the afternoon, while her mother visited a friend or read a book, her father listened to the football game on the radio, drawing elaborate diagrams on paper as the announcer described their positions in order to see where the players were on the field. It would be peaceful to be sure, and predictable. But it would not be *her* life.

It was all too much of a muddle and too weighty a decision for August. To avoid thinking, Helen started taking long naps in the afternoons. And when she woke and the evening breeze arrived to clear away the warm afternoon, she took warm baths. She visited Clementine regularly and tried to be useful by shopping for her, but there wasn't much to do, as the neighbors had that very well organized. Clementine was rapidly returning to her old self, and the second time Helen visited Clementine, she had Rose's engagement dress laid out on her bed and was figuring out how to repair it. With her steady gaze fixed on Helen, she solemnly promised not to do any ironing when the temperature was over eighty degrees.

Once, Helen went with Rose and Fred out to the Jersey shore to lie on the sand and play in the water. But the two of them were so in love and excited about life that it was almost sickening. 'Three's a crowd' had never felt truer. She knew there were people to whose homes she could invite herself, and she could try to build relationships, but it all just seemed like so much effort. The truth was, she missed Thomas. Rose asked her as much one day, her head cocked quizzically. “I don’t know,” she muttered quietly, avoiding Rose’s gaze. But Helen did know, and she didn’t know what to do about it.

In the end, through procrastination and avoidance, she decided not to decide anything in particular until September. September was a much better month for beginning things. Wasn't that when the Jewish New Year was? And weren't they God's people? And wouldn't He know? And anyway, she reasoned, it was only at the end of

September that her finances would really begin to press and she would finally be forced to do one thing or another.

So the last of August passed, and Helen tried to count her blessings that she at least didn't have to wear stockings and pumps in a hot office all day. Rose's engagement party was in a week, and Helen told herself that afterward she would definitely think seriously about the future. In the meantime, she determined for this week to assist Rose in whatever way she could.

Chapter 50

The week passed more slowly than Helen had hoped. It turned out there wasn't much she could do to help with the party preparations, as Mrs. Whitaker had everything well in hand. The awaited day finally arrived, full of clear blue skies and bright promise.

In the early afternoon, Helen drove out with Fred and Rose in the back of Fred's car. High Hills Country Club spread out like an emerald carpet on the banks of the Hudson River. Green and white awnings stretched out from stately white brick buildings decorated with green shutters and red geraniums. Everything was as close to perfect as Mrs. Whitaker could manage it. Rose was beautiful in the dress Clementine had made for her. Helen wore a simple blue summer dress she'd had for years. It had only recently occurred to her that she was apathetic about attending such a social event with nothing new to wear. She marveled as she recalled all her efforts getting ready for the ball, having a dress made by Clementine; it all seemed so very long ago. Even if she had wanted to buy something new, she didn't have the money to spend. But somehow, it seemed fitting to her now subdued state of being. As they stepped out of the car, before parents and relatives pressed around them, Rose turned to her, her eyes smiling.

"Helen, you look just lovely," she said simply.

"Thank you, Rose." She looked at her friend, full of affection. "But today is your day. *You* are the stunning beauty. I am so grateful that I can be here with you."

"Helen's right, you know. Rose, you are perfect," said Fred. He gazed at his fiancée with shining eyes, and then he grinned at Helen. "And her best friend is lovely."

Fred's words caught Helen's heart. Fred had called her Rose's best friend. She looked across, and Rose smiled at her with joy and affection.

***

The party was a late afternoon lunch fading into cocktail hour. Into the country club drifted a slice of beautiful society, friends and family of the Whitakers coming to celebrate their beloved only child. Helen had the impression that she was surrounded by a garden full of colorful flowers, all lovely, perfect, stately, and pleasant. At first she didn't think she would know anyone besides Rose's parents. But here and there in the group of beautiful people she found familiar faces. Aunt Martha recognized her and came over to say hello, her loud voice audible above everyone else's.

"Well, Helen, how the heck are ya?" She went on without waiting for Helen's answer. "This Fred fella ain't half bad, don't ya think? At any rate, it's probably too late now."

Helen saw a few heads turn toward the loud voice and stare, presumably some of Fred's relatives. "When's the wedding, anyway? None of this waiting around forever business, I hope. George and I waited, and then off to the war he went and got killed. Nope. We should have gotten married right away and at least have had a few days of happiness. All this modern waiting, it's a bad idea. Once they've set their minds to it, might as well go through on the spot. The next time a man proposes to me, I'm going to march him right down to the church that very day." Aunt Martha finished her soliloquy and then nodded smugly with her eyes closed. That was all there was to say about that.

Clementine was there, too, trying successfully to blend into the background. Helen found her sitting near a corner of the terrace under a grape arbor, watching the other guests and eyeing their gowns. The grapes on the arbor were growing large and purple, almost ready to harvest. Beyond Rose's immediate family, no one knew Clementine's exact connection beyond "family friend." With their usual grace and calm, Mr. and Mrs. Whitaker had accepted Clementine's part in their circle, quietly acknowledging the role she had played in bringing them their precious daughter. Since she didn't threaten them with replacement in Rose's affections, they were not on the defensive and were slowly adjusting to the change in their family dynamic.

Clementine stood up as she watched Helen approach. She wore a simple dress compared to most of those floating around them, but she looked a perfectly framed picture. This new role as friend and mentor to her long-lost daughter did much for her, a healthy glow on her cheeks and a joyful smile on her lips. Clementine's well-tailored dress in a deep shade of violet was striking as she stood under the arbor of purple grapes. They embraced, and Helen sat down next to her friend.

"I was just thinking, Helen, how it was just a year ago that you came to me about another party. How my life has changed since then," said Clementine.

"My life feels different, too. I think a year ago I would have preferred to be out there in the middle of all those lovely people. Now I think it seems nicer here." She smiled at her friend, then added, uncertainly, "You don't regret it, do you Clementine? Should I have just left things alone, like..." *like Thomas said*, she had been going to say. She swallowed. "...like they were?"

"Regret? No, Helen, not at all. Sometimes it is difficult to adjust to something new in life, but I don't regret it at all. I am blessed, I know. Not everyone would feel the same way toward me as Rose does, but she has good parents, and they raised her with honesty and grace. After all those years, I would have been happy just to know who and where she was. I never could have imagined being a part of all of this." She raised her hand and indicated the party, the beautiful swirling flowers of people, with Rose at the center of it.

They watched her from afar, the two of them in the grape arbor. A cluster of grapes dangled temptingly just above Helen and she stood up and plucked a grape. Without thinking, she popped it into her mouth and crunched it between her teeth. It was huge and juicy and tart. Almost completely ripe, but not quite. The food at the party had all been delicious: smoked salmon, imported French cheeses, foie gras on canapés, all so well prepared, so sophisticated, that this grape almost sent a shock through Helen with its wildness, its freshness, its jolt of sour with an enormous promise of sweet just around the corner. It was startling, and almost immediately upon swallowing it she longed for another. Her hand felt the urge to reach up for another grape, a desire so strong that it overcame the shame of eating the party decorations.

The wild taste lingered on her tongue, and suddenly Helen wanted to be away from the party. She wanted to be away from the city, away from all the people. She excused herself from Clementine and slipped away along a path that ran behind the arbor and led from the terrace through the flower gardens above the riverbank. She walked slowly through the gardens where hollyhocks, roses, dahlias, zinnias, sunflowers and daisies all danced together in the warm breeze. On the far side of the garden the green lawn sloped gently down to the river's edge. On the other side of the river the sun made its descent toward hills on the horizon, lost in the golden haze of brilliant light. Near to the river's edge there was a bench, and in that instant Helen wanted nothing more intensely than to sit on that bench, alone, in all that brightness. *He will make your righteousness shine like the sun.* The phrase flowed through her mind as she tried to look into the fiery ball. She had heard it read in church with Thomas. But what did it mean? She hesitated a moment and then started down the slope. She wondered about walking on the grass and whether she was risking her ankle once again, but then she realized the footing was firmer than she expected.

She sat on the bench, closed her eyes and felt the warmth of the sun. Her life was not anything like she had once wanted it to be. Nor was it what she knew it should be. She knew that she herself wasn't who she wanted to be. But for now, in this moment, she wasn't afraid of the future. She was simply grateful for the part she had played in the lives of those she cared about. She sat on the bench until the sun went down and the golden light in the west faded and the first stars came out.

Chapter 51

Monday morning was the first day at Rose's school, and she left the apartment early. Helen slept late and then wandered out to the kitchen. She made herself a cup of coffee and sat down at the table to drink it. There was an envelope on the table with her own name on it in Rose's handwriting. She took a sip and opened the letter. *Dear Helen,* the letter began,

You took a risk in introducing me to Clementine, and in doing so you gave me a doorway to someone who is meant to be a beautiful part of my life. Now I'm taking a risk and hope that I am doing the same for you. I called Thomas, and told him all that you've done for Clementine this past month, and for me as well. He regrets ever giving you any 'stupid deadline'—his words. Helen, don't let the mistakes of your past sabotage your future. Be forgiven and move forward. At least go and see him. You've become a better friend than I ever imagined. I only want the best for you—I hope this will be part of that. Forgive me if I'm wrong.

With great affection, Rose

From the envelope Helen pulled out a train ticket—Grand Central Station to South Deerfield, Massachusetts. Helen stared at it a long time. Then, with a shy smile growing broader on her face every second, she got up and went to pack her bags.

Acknowledgments

Thank you to those who helped make the dream of this book a reality over years and continents. To God, who gives the ability to read and write and love words. To my mother-in-law, Brida, for the trip to New York that inspired the idea for this story and for many memories of her childhood in Switzerland that found their way into the book. To my late mother, Janice, whose letters home provided me with the character of Helen. To Marijo who long ago nourished my dreams of writing and more recently was my first non-related reader and editor. To my editor Rebecca for her excellent wordsmithing. To Delphine, who lent me her fireside by which to edit. To Kerry, Leigh, Noelle, Rene and Sheri who helped me keep at it all this time by wanting to read the finished product. To Alia who wants a French translation. To Laura and Shar and the Black Book Collective for making me want to keep on writing. To my brother, Chip, who always spoke about my book using the word "when" not "if" which is an incalculable difference. To Peter at BespokeBookCovers for my wonderful cover design. To my daughters, Marina and

Evangeline, who read my first versions and gave invaluable input. To my sons, Peter and Zarli for putting up with my hours of "working on the novel." To my beloved husband Manu, who always believed in me. And finally, thanks to Helen, who wanted her story to be written.

Made in the USA
San Bernardino, CA
23 January 2017